My Heaven

Holding On To Heaven

My Heaven
By
Melyssa Winchester

Copyright © 2014 Melyssa Winchester

Cover Design by Pressmaster @ Shutterstock

This book is dedicated to my son, Caleb. If it wasn't for you, I wouldn't know what true love, in all its forms, really is. I love you and no matter how old you get, I always will.

Authors Note

This was to be the way that Holding On To Heaven (Love United Series #1) was originally plotted to end. It is recommended that before reading this story, that you go back and familiarize yourself with that story in an effort to understand this one fully. It is also recommended that the epilogue as it appears in Holding On To Heaven be ignored as it pertains to the original series as a whole (5 books).

Prologue

Light Over Darkness

Gabriel

In the last two months I have gone against not only my father's orders, but that of Heaven itself more times than ever before. It has all been for the light known as Serenity. While there are instances I would never repeat should I ever have the chance to redo them, for the most part I would always do what I have done as it pertains to her. Not because of my feelings, but because apart from all of that she is special.

One of a kind.

After securing my brothers cooperation, each of us agreeing to use our powers to block out our father as much as possible, we began to plan what we would do upon our entry into Lucifer's grand design. I filled everyone in on where he was located, what the master plan will be and just what we would be walking into. We were all aware of the risks, but this is something none of us could back away from.

It was time to come face to face with Lucifer.

We spent centuries of time away from him, only interacting with the lower demons he employs. Each of us has a great deal of love for our brother, going so far as to not give up on him after he had been cast out. We have always wanted a better resolution to the problems he and Father face and we still had hope, even now, that one day they would come together again. We want to believe the best of him, choosing to hold onto the belief that he is just misguided.

What he is doing to Serenity; that is not the Lucifer we know and love. No, this is what became of him when he thought his entire family to have turned on him. If we could just tap into maybe we could save him as well as Ryan and Serenity from the fate that beheld them.

Which led us to where we stand now.

All four brothers, standing side by side, blades at the ready, preparing ourselves for whatever possible scenario we might walk into the minute we go through the chapel doors.

I can only hope that we are not too late. Lucifer had taken precautions against us, as there were markings placed all around the church set to disallow entrance, but it wasn't enough to stop us. Uriel, being an expert at getting into places that entities of our sort are normally forbidden from, dropped the magic easily and once he did, we executed our plan.

Michael and Raphael began to make quick work of the demons guarding the door, using their blades fast and efficiently, obliterating his army so that no trace was left behind. Once done, they turned to me, and motioned for me to move forward.

I am at the center of the plan. Without me and what I am about to do, we might not make it out of here alive. I have to make sure that no matter how horrible the situation is for her when I enter, I stay on task. There is only one chance at this, which means no room for mistakes.

I am the one that has to get Lucifer's attention. Distract him long enough for Uriel to wipe the brand from Serenity so that we can get her and the demon away from Lucifer and certain death.

Standing outside the chapel doors, I mentally prepare myself for what happens next.

"Does it strike anyone as poetic that Lucifer chose a church to do this in? I always knew there were parts of him the darkness would not change and it appears I was right." Michael stated as he situates himself in seclusion as I place my hand on the handles of the large wooden door.

"He always did have a flare for the dramatic. This is no different then what he did in Heaven." Uriel responded, his face frozen in determination.

"Are you all in position?" I whisper, scanning around me and taking in all three brothers, locked into their spots, their faces blank slates.

"Let the party begin." Raphael muttered quietly from his corner behind the right side door.

Pulling back the door with my hand, wide enough for me and the girth of my now glowing wings to make it all the way inside. The deeper I enter into the room the more I took in the devastation around me.

Lucifer is bending over Serenity, whose still body lays unmoving above a dark covered mattress, stains of blood visible on her pale arms. I swallow my feelings as I realize that he had already drained her, making us too late for her to be saved. Off to the right of her, I see the demon, also lying in a pool of his own blood, a hole visible in the clothing he wore, his once clear eyes vacant and cold, with only a little remaining spec of black within them. The remains of his demon self.

"You always were the smart one, Gabriel." Lucifer boasted as he moved forward, his expansive size calling my attention away from the cold bodies I witness around me. "How you managed to get past my warding spells is beyond me, but I cannot say I'm not happy that you did. It has been far too long little brother."

"What you have done here, Lucifer I cannot allow to continue. You have forsaken the very part of yourself that we as your brothers believed to still be intact. You must be punished."

"Look around you dear brother. You are too late. The plan is a complete success. In a few short minutes I will possess the rotting carcass of my most trusted confidante and I will be completely unstoppable. It is of no consequence to me now that you believe me to be evil."

From the looks of the destruction around me I knew there is no argument I can make. Between Serenity's stiff and pale body, to that of the very demon that had most likely died trying to protect her, it did appear as if he had everything under control. Except I knew different. He had not planned on the arrival of his brothers.

"I will not allow you to take Ryan as your host and neither will the others."

For the first time in forever, I witness a look of shock appear across my brother's face as his eyes grow wide and his lips grew tight.

"Others? Who has agreed to meet their demise along with you today?"

From behind me I heard them move from their location and felt the ground shake as they all moved forward as a unit. The human saying of there being strength in numbers is no more real than it is in this moment now. The most powerful of Heaven all in one room, ready to take down the fallen one.

"If it isn't a family reunion! How sweet. I'm amazed you could get that one there out of Heaven at all. That is quite the accomplishment, Gabriel." He replies with a smirk as he points to Raphael.

"Where we may not see eye to eye on most things, in this regard we do and we are here together as one to stop you from going through with what you have planned to do."

"How do you propose to do that, Gabriel? As I said, the stage has been set. Even though I am wounded, I still hold more than enough power to take you all down."

I hear the smash before I see it, as the bottle flew up and over my own head and landed squarely at Lucifer's feet, breaking with a crash into hundreds of small shards, the liquid from inside pouring out all around him.

Before he has time to react, using every bit of the power I still had at my disposal, I shape the fire ball in my hands, building it more with every movement my hands make until it is large enough to cover his body the minute it reacts with the holy oil.

With one more burst of strength I pushed it toward him, and back away as it collides with its target. Within seconds, Lucifer went up in flames, the fire ball mixing together with the oil and creating a wide open circle of fire around his now burning body.

"You are only postponing the inevitable, young angel." he shouts through the fire, barely legible through the sound of the flames crackling as they grew higher around him.

"Maybe so, but all I need is a brief interruption." I state as I motion with my hands for Uriel to begin his part of the plan.

I watch in awe as Uriel makes his way to where Serenity lies and as her body begins to glow under his power, I know that soon the branding would be gone and we would be able to remove her from this place. Even if I arrived too late, at least when it is all said and done, I would have gotten her body back where it belongs.

In Heaven.

"Saving the girl. How typical of you. Too bad I don't care about her; she was just a means to an end. An end that as you can see has definitely been reached."

Before I could respond, I heard Uriel's voice loud and clear in my mind.

"She is still alive. We must move her now before he learns of his mistake."

"Do it. Take her home."

Focusing my attention back on Lucifer I watch as Uriel lifts her into his arms and within seconds vanishes out of the chapel. Releasing the breath I had been holding I smiled at back at him.

"Michael, you must remove Ryan from here before the oil burns out. There isn't much time left."

As Michael and Raphael made their way over to where Ryan lay motionless, I watch as Lucifer steps out around the ball of fire that until now he had been trapped in.

"You will do nothing of the sort."

As he made his way toward me, I summon the blade to my hand, preparing for the fight. How he walked out of the holy fire I did not know, but I couldn't let that little surprise stop me. As much as I do not want to be the one to kill my brother I know now that it might be the only way to make it out of this alive. He is stronger than I originally gave him credit for.

"Do you not see, Gabriel? I can walk from the holy fire practically unscathed. I can surely deal with a silly blade of heaven. You know Father only used those as props anyway."

He reached out and grabbed me, lifting me from the ground by my neck, squeezing harder the higher he lifted me into the air. Michael, who had left Raphael to deal with the moving of the demon turned and shot a blast of lightning from his palms, hitting Lucifer in the back, releasing his hold. As I hit the ground, the blade clanging against the cement floor beside me, I dived toward it, as my brother grabbed tightly onto my leg in an attempt to stop me.

Kicking him off, I turn and sit up and much the way Michael had done, I grew a ball of energy in my hands, whipping it toward him, knocking him completely backwards until his body lay still.

"Now! Get Ryan out of here now!" I screamed, again turning my attention back to the blade, securing it in my grasp before bringing myself up by the wings to a standing position above Lucifer. As I stare down at him, knowing at any moment he could get back up, I see the weak look in his eyes and the blade marks protruding from his chest. There is no sign of blood yet I knew that the marks had damaged him.

As Michael and Raphael vanished from sight, the body of the demon disappearing with them, I breathe out one last sigh of relief before turning my attention back to the brother lying broken at my feet.

"Your plan was flawless, Lucifer. You really did think of everything. You just did the one thing we all expected you to do."

"What—is—that?" He asks as he struggles for each breath to get the words out. What I could only hope were his final ones.

"You thought you had it all figured out of course. You let your head get bigger than the rest of you. By the power of

Heaven, this is where your darkness ends. You will never see the light again."

I plunge the blade deep into him and watch as the black blood slowly begins to pour from his chest, staining the ground below. As I watch him inhale his last breath, content that I am the one here for his final moments, I whisper a prayer for the dying, placing one final kiss on his brow before bowing my head and apparating.

Darkness has a way of creeping up on you, making its presence known before you even realize it's happened. It takes over your life, turning you into the very thing you have been sworn to destroy. That will not happen because today is a new day. The darkness would no longer have the chance to reign supreme.

Today the light has won.

Chapter One

A New Reality

Gabriel

Things will never be the same again.

What should be a time of great celebration, all of Heaven rejoicing in the ending of the darkness, is marred by events that took place before. Where we should be celebrating, we are in mourning, not only for the brother we have lost, but for the half demon that had given his life in order to prove his allegiance to the light.

Ryan McGregor, from the very moment of his creation had been put on one path, never to deviate from it. He was to come to Serenity, befriend her and turn her to the darkness. Lucifer waited for her eagerly, more than ready to take her as his bride and strip her of the very life force that runs strongly through her veins.

The half demon had chosen a different path, one guided by the love he felt for the heavenly ball of light and in the end had gone to his death in an effort to save her. Losing him this way, arriving too late to prevent the sacrifice he made, it cannot be undone and no matter how much I ache for a chance to do everything over again, putting more trust in him instead of assuming him to be as dark as the man that raised him, I cannot.

He earned his redemption, but only after he had been lost. His sacrifice will never be forgotten, but even knowing how right his decision had been, it does not make what I have to do now easier.

Serenity was removed before the battle reached its end and just as Uriel alluded to in the church, she is alive and well, her body mending due to the healing light my brothers have surrounded her with. She had also made the ultimate sacrifice and just as it is with the half demon, hers will never be forgotten or overlooked.

She had been the only one to see the light buried so deeply within Ryan and in an effort to save and bring him back to the light where she knew he belonged, she had chosen to embrace the life Lucifer mapped out for her. It was never meant to be her destiny to join the darkness, but he had seen fit to lock her into it once she had given him her acceptance.

It was written that she would be the one to end Lucifer's reign and I have no doubt that if she had been strong enough after what she endured in the church, she would have done just that, not only for what he put her through, but for Ryan as well. She wanted nothing more than to do the right thing by the half demon, though now it seems to have all been for naught.

Ryan has been lost to us, despite our every attempt at bringing him back. Michael had immediately gone to work, even going so far as to reach out to the demonic side of him, attempting to use it to bring him back to life, but it was to no avail. He had passed on in the church, of that I am sure, but now that we know for certain that there is nothing more we can do to return him to the way he had been before, we are left with informing those that are still unaware.

I am left to inform Serenity that the man she went through hell for is dead.

I make no claims at understanding the connection that appeared between them, something that if the boy had lived, we would have wanted to study and learn more about, but there can be no mistaking that she did indeed care for him a great deal, willing to put her own life on the line in order to save him and make all of Heaven see the light.

I do not relish doing this.

It is with a heavy heart that I stand before her with Michael standing watch as she heals. It is only a matter of time before she wakes up, no doubt asking for information as it pertains to Ryan and it is then that I would have to level her with the hardest truth that she has ever had to face.

Finding out that she was made of Heaven and that everything she has been experiencing from the young age of five all had a very important meaning, would seem like nothing compared to telling her that the man she had given her heart to, the very man she married had perished.

My heart is made heavier by the knowledge that she would not be alone in the loss she felt. I may not care for the boy the way she did, but in my own way, I am also experiencing a loss like no other before. She had lost Ryan and in the end, I had lost Lucifer. Father and son and now my beloved and I are left the pick up the pieces of our loss.

It is something I do not think I will ever be able to do. How does one move on from a loss such as this? If I am unable to get over what I did ending Lucifer, how can I expect Serenity to do the same with the half demon?

Sharing a bond with her, it is supposed to be beautiful and bathed in the purest light, not leveled in pain and agony the way that it is now.

"As hard as I know this is going to be for you Gabriel, it has to be done. I know that you want to spare her the pain of losing Ryan, but if you do so it will only damage her more in the end."

Michael does not need to remind me of the facts. I am more than aware of what I must do, but it does not mean I have to like it. Being the one to tell Serenity of this, I am not sure how wise a move that is. It is no secret the way I felt about him. I do believe it would come easier hearing it from Michael or even Father above me.

I am afraid that in telling her, I will only make her despise me more.

"You cannot believe that."

"Is this the point at which you give me the speech again, Michael?"

"I am not sure what speech you are referring to, but if it is the one where I believe that you are in with your train of thought than yes."

"How can you say that I am wrong? You are aware of the way she felt about me before she agreed to Lucifer's plan. The moment I tell her that Ryan gave up his life in order to save hers, she is only going to think worse of me."

"You are so misguided. Serenity is made of the exact same light as you are, brother. Surely you have not forgotten this in the midst of the pity party you are throwing yourself. I am aware of what you believe, but I do believe I know that girl better than you do. She will be heartbroken, of that I am sure, but she could never hate you."

"I hear what you are saying, but Michael, I do believe you should be the one to tell her."

It may not be the way Father wanted things handled, but I would not change my feelings on the matter. Michael needs to be the one to do this because I could not bring myself to hurt her again.

She has already been through enough.

Serenity

No.

He's lying to me. This angel with the hair so light it could almost be considered white is doing what the angels have been doing from the very beginning. Lying and keeping things from me.

There's no way that Ryan is gone.

No.

I refuse to believe it. He's just been through a lot. They're keeping him from me because the demon side of him came out and they're worried about my safety. When I'm completely healed and able to get up and back to my life, they would let me see him and things would go back to normal.

Ryan wouldn't leave me, not after everything we went through together in order to make everything right with the world, Heaven and with us. We haven't even had a real shot at a life together. Him being ripped away from me now, it's just not possible.

This is all just a sick and twisted joke.

"Serenity. I wish that I could tell you that what you are thinking is correct, but I cannot. It is as I have said. Ryan, in his attempt to save you, perished."

"NO!" I scream, no longer caring where I am or who is around to hear me. I refuse to listen to any more of this. This angel, whoever he is, is lying to me and if I have to keep on screaming at him until he stops, I will. "Ryan is NOT DEAD!"

He wouldn't leave me. He loves me too much.

"I know it is hard to process. You cannot bring your mind around to the truth when your heart is so deeply involved, but Serenity, in order for you to heal completely, you need to come to terms with this. The longer you push it away, focusing instead on the make believe, the longer it will take you to recover from what Lucifer put you through."

Lucifer.

All of this is happening right now because of him. He put all of this in motion and he's the reason the angel is lying to me now. I bet they're working together in order to make me believe something that I will just never believe in.

"If this works the way I intend sweet angel, you will not be going anywhere. I will not drain you completely. I would never do that. I will leave you with just enough blood so that you can begin to heal. I cannot offer much time to do so, but I'm hoping to buy enough so you can make it out of here safely and alive. Please trust and believe in that. I will not let you die, not while there is still breath in my lungs."

His voice filling my head, his final words haunting me as I do everything I can to block out the angel delivering the blow. I focus on how he sounded, the words he said, the ones that if what I'm hearing now is true, he would never speak again.

There's just no way after everything he had done in order to keep me safe that he would have done anything that would take him away from me. He would have been fighting to be with me. I know that he didn't think he was a match for Lucifer, but I knew better. There is no one that can take on the devil and win more than Ryan McGregor.

I refuse to believe this.

My heart is starting to believe in the angels words despite my deep seeded desire not to. I can feel the loss of him deep in my chest, the ache that resides there, knowing that there is a part of me missing. He might not have a bond with me the way Gabriel and Graham do, but his impact had gone much deeper. I loved him with everything I had.

"You can feel it."

"It doesn't matter what I feel because it's not true."

"Serenity, I am aware that you do not know me, but I can assure you, I am not, nor will I ever work with my fallen brother. I understand you are having a difficult time coming to terms with the truth, but I was the one that got him out of the church and spent days attempting to save him. I wanted nothing more than to bring the boy back to you, to all of us as he earned his redemption."

Ignoring the ache in my chest at the mere mention of him earning his redemption, I focus instead on the other words. He had been the one to work on Ryan? He spent days trying to save him?

"Yes. Gabriel noticed the boy in the corner of the church and asked me and Uriel to remove him. At the time we knew he was gravely injured but had no idea the extent of it. It was only when we got him through the gates that it became apparent."

"Lucifer stabbed him?"

"No. At first we believed that to be the case. I am of the belief that Ryan, going against him the way he had been, finally drove my brother to a point that he could not turn away from, but I was wrong. Accessing Ryan's final moments, I learned the truth."

"The truth being?"

"He was indeed controlled by Lucifer to pick up the blade and injure himself, but it was not supposed to be a fatal blow. Ryan plunged the blade deeper than even my fallen brother intended and took his own life in an effort to save yours."

"He killed himself to save me?"

"It appears that way yes."

"He made the wrong choice. He never should've saved me at all. Without him, I might as well be dead."

Chapter Two

Moving On

Graham

I'm not sure how much more of this I can take.

She's been like this for weeks now. From the minute Gabriel brought her back and she stepped back into her life, it's just been one forced and repeated motion after another. There's no mistaking that Serenity is here, but the one that is going through the motions isn't the one I know at all.

After going a little over a week with no word from the angels or her, I had nothing to go on with what happened in Green Haven. Gabriel ditched me after my failed attempt to get her free of the choice she made and he hadn't come back since. Once he did, he filled me in on everything that went down and that's what I'm faced with now.

It has taken her a lot longer to heal than the angels expected, but she's back now and just like every other day since they brought her back to me, she's repeating the same torturous routine. She wakes in the morning, makes her way from her dorm at the same exact time, walking to class, never stopping once in between.

When I first got here, she was travelling with Emma, but ever since she walked away from me that day at the coffee shop and chose to side with Ryan, she's been completely alone. She might be rooming with Emma, they might even still be as close as they've always been, but when she's out around the rest of the campus, Emma is nowhere in sight. It's always just her and that tells me a lot more than talking ever could.

Serenity has always been this way. From the second she moved in across the street from me, she's kept whatever she's feeling to herself. It took me months to learn what she really thought about me after she moved in and I made my stupid visit welcoming her to the neighborhood. That's how close to the vest she keeps everything, even the things that mean nothing.

When the plan failed, I decided on going back to Green Haven for the duration. I came to Stephenville with one purpose and I failed, so armed with the reality of her choice, I was more than ready to go back to my life before Serenity had been thrown back into it. The visit from Gabriel, it changed everything and here I am, ready to throw myself in her path again. Only this time, it's for a completely different reason.

I came here before with the sole purpose of connecting with her, helping Gabriel to prevent her from making the choice she ended up making. I also came back because despite all my cheap talk of moving on, I never did. We had unfinished business and I couldn't walk away until it was dealt with. The truth is, Serenity and me, we're always going to have unfinished business because I'm always going to love her.

This time, I'm here for her, but I'm also here for me and it's got nothing to do with the way I feel. We've always needed each other and armed with the truth about what we mean to each other, I'm even more determined to be what she needs now. A friend. The one person in the world that even though he might not totally understand, wouldn't push her to be something she's not.

Of course Gabriel makes it out to be something else entirely, but he's guided by his own bond so I can't fault him. He just needs to realize that we have different ways of looking at this, no matter what he said to me the night he came back and told me everything.

Rinsing the cutting board, lining it up with the other dishes, I reach over and grab the pot off the stovetop. Placing it on the counter, I turn toward the fridge and that's when the light hits

me. A light that I haven't seen in over a week and one I never thought I was going to see again.

Gabriel's here and just like before, he's standing in my kitchen, his expression grave.

"My apologies for popping in like this, but there is much that I need to discuss with you."

Cordial as always, just the way God intended when he made him no doubt.

"Don't need to apologize man. It's not like I was doing anything all that important anyway. Pretty sure putting together a box of mac and cheese is pretty low on the list of importance."

I grin at him, but his expression remains locked in place. Whatever he's here to talk to me about, it doesn't take a brain surgeon to realize it's as serious as it gets. I just hope that this time he doesn't leave anything out. Finding out everything after the fact last time was bad enough.

"Well, you gonna tell me why you're here or leave me to guess?"

"This visit should have come sooner. For that I need to apologize, but much has happened since we last spoke and that took precedence."

Serenity, that's what he's getting at. He won't say her name though, which makes me curious to know exactly what it is about her that he's having such a hard time getting out. What happened after he ditched me and headed back to the church?

"You are correct, this is about Serenity. Things have taken a turn that I did not anticipate and I am here to again ask for your help."

"Not agreeing to anything until you tell me everything."

"I know you do not trust me and I intend to tell you everything you need to know, but Graham, you may want to sit down. What you are about to hear is not going to be pretty."

She was forced into marrying a half demon because she thought she needed to save him. It didn't get much worse than that, at least from where I'm sitting, but with the way he continues to stare through me instead of at me, I do as he says and slide my body down into the chair.

"Serenity did indeed follow through with the marriage to Ryan. It is the ritual that took place after that brings me here now."

"Ritual? You mean, the part where Lucifer wanted her dead?"

"Yes. Ryan did as he was forced to do, but managed to find a loophole in the way Lucifer commanded him and was able to ensure Serenity's survival."

"She's alive?"

"If you call the way she has been living, being alive, then yes."

"What does that mean?"

"In order for me to explain that, I need to continue telling you what happened."

"All ears man."

"Ryan was able to keep her alive long enough for Uriel to get her out of the church and back to Heaven. What we were unable to do was save him. Ryan perished in the aftermath despite our every attempt to prevent it."

Now I get why he wanted me to sit. Hearing that Serenity survived what she went through, it made me want to scream from rooftops, but just as quickly as the urge came it was replaced by something else when he told me what happened next.

Ryan McGregor, the half demon hybrid that put her on this path in the first place, the very guy that she told me she had feelings for a little over a week ago, he's dead and judging by the agonizing look on the archangels face now, Serenity knew about it, which made his reason for being here make sense.

"It's a stupid question, but how is she taking it?"

"She hasn't spoken a word since Michael informed her of Ryan's passing and all that we did to prevent it. It is as if she has locked herself up tight and will not let anyone in."

"That's exactly what she did."

His head dips and despite the seriousness of the conversation, I can't help smiling. Even with all the knowledge he has about our history, he still manages to be amazed that I know her as well as I do.

"Look man, you've spent enough time around her. You know how she is. She doesn't do emotional. You telling her that the guy she just went through hell for is dead, it made her shut down. It's too much. She's doing what she's always done."

"Which is precisely why I'm here."

"You want me to try and get through to her, don't you?"

He nods and I think about what the nod really means. The last time he stood here and asked me for help with her, he'd been doing it because he screwed up and knew that in the end I would be the one person that could help him fix it. He used me in an effort to get into her good graces again, even if wanting to protect her had been the truth. There's nothing stopping him from repeating it all over again even though things are different.

"What aren't you telling me?"

"I am not sure what you mean."

"You kept things from me before, so what are you keeping from me now?"

"Nothing. I can't go back and fix the way I handled the situation in the past Graham. I can only assure you that this time, you are aware of everything that you need to be."

"In other words, what you deem fit to tell me?"

"No. You know as much as I do, as Michael does. I would like to tell you that you know as much as my father, but we both know that would be the lie."

"Where is she now?"

"Heaven. She will be there for some time yet. There is much that is needed to be done in terms of healing before she can come back to her life here."

"Well then, do what you need to do for her on your end and when she's ready to come home, leave the rest to me. I won't let her go through this alone."

"Graham, I feel there is much I need to say before I take my leave."

"Is there more that I don't know?"

"Yes."

"Then spill it. If I'm gonna help you again, I wanna know it all."

"Lucifer was not the one to end Ryan's life. He controlled the outcome, but it was Ryan who made the ultimate sacrifice."

Did I just hear him right? Is he telling me that Ryan killed himself?

"In a manner of speaking, yes. Ryan, in an effort to right the wrongs done; the path he put her on by agreeing to the plan at all, took his own life in an effort to save hers. In order to save us all."

Jesus Christ.

"Please refrain from doing that. You know how I feel about it."

"Does she know that he did that for her?"

"Yes."

"Well, that makes everything that much harder."

"What do you mean?"

"I know you guys don't know a whole lot about the way humans are, like how we act when there are feelings involved, but it's not rocket science, Gabriel. She cared about the guy enough to die for him. Waking up, finding out you're alive while the person you were supposed to save isn't is bad enough, but finding out that he killed himself to protect you? It's ten times worse."

"I am still not sure what you mean."

This is frustrating. What I said, if I was talking to anyone else, they would get it but with this archangel, the one that seems to feel more than I assumed a being like him could, it's not getting through at all. I'm running head first into a brick wall with him, repeatedly and there's not a whole lot I can do about it.

"She's blaming herself, man. You wanna know why none of you can break through her walls? Why she's pulled away so deep inside herself? Look no further than what you just told me. He killed himself to save her. She thinks she caused this."

When an angel realizes something, it's pretty cool to watch. They're surrounded by such a bright light already that when their common sense kicks in and they begin to understand, it really is like a light bulb going off above them. If it's possible,

Gabriel realizing what I'm telling him, has made him even brighter.

"Serenity did nothing of the sort."

"Obviously. She made the choice to save Ryan and he made the choice to do whatever it took to save her. All she's going to see is that because of the way he felt about her, he did this. If she didn't have this supposed destiny to begin with, Ryan would still be here."

"I understand the human condition. I can even sympathize with it easier than my brothers, but this I cannot grasp. It makes no sense to me that any human, especially Serenity would put that kind of pressure on themselves."

"Welcome to grief and loss 101. You don't get it, but I do. I've been through this shit with my mom. Losing her, knowing that it's coming at some point, it twists you up inside so bad that reality can't break through."

The room falls silent as he seems to really think about what I'm telling him, what I've just admitted about myself. His head is bowed now so that I'm unable to see just how much my words have affected him and after waiting as patiently as I can for a few minutes, I clear my throat in an effort to remind him that he's not alone.

"I give you a lot to think about?"

"Yes, you have. You have also proven to me that I did the right thing coming here today. Graham, I know it is most inconvenient but I need to know. Will you do what is needed to bring her back to me—us?"

I don't miss the slip near the end. I know how he feels about Serenity and I'm pretty damn sure it's identical or close to what I feel. I also know that it's got nothing to do with some stupid bond that Heaven seems to think we share. It's more basic than that, more real. I might not know all there is to know about what it is they share between them and I'm not sure how I feel about it even if I did know, but right now none of that matters. All that does matter is saving Serenity, this time for good.

"Yeah I will, but Gabriel, this; what I'm doing here. It's got nothing at all to do with you or Heaven or what your father wants. I'm not doing it for you. I'm doing it for her."

"Because you love her?"

"No. Love, what I feel for her, it can't play a part in this. Selfishness is what got us into this mess to begin with. If we're gonna do right by Serenity than we've got to do things differently."

"How do you plan on doing that? It is not as if you can just turn your feelings off. The bond will not let you."

"You're right, I can't. I'm in love with her and I was before I even knew about the bond. I've got something stronger than the bond though and that's what I'm gonna use to bring her back."

"What would that be?"

"Understanding and a strong urge to do the right thing. She wasn't meant to die in the church and she's not meant to die now. It's not about what we share between us, what could possibly happen in the future. None of that matters. All that does matter is doing what I promised her years ago that I would do."

"Which is?"

"I would never give up on her and I mean it now as much as I did then. She's never going to go through this or anything else alone again."

~*~*~

She might not be ready to face it or me again, but I meant what I said to Gabriel that night. Serenity wouldn't be going through all of this, what I know she's forcing down, alone. Not anymore. I made her that promise when I was a stupid kid with a crush, but just because the circumstances may have changed drastically, it didn't make it any less true.

Whether she likes it or not, I'm back and this time I'm not leaving her. She's stuck with me and watching her cut across the lawn now, my gaze locked on her as she passes by the tree I'm leaned against, I know the time for watching her, keeping up with her routines and feeling her out is over.

It's time for me to see Serenity again and this time, succeed where I failed. It's time to save her, but this time not from Lucifer and the dark destiny he has waiting for her.

This time I have to save her from herself.

Chapter Three

Dear Agony

Serenity

"I prayed that someone going through this would find me, so I wouldn't have to go it alone. I was so tired of being the weird kid that talked to dead people."
"Did anything ever come of it?"
"Yeah, something did."
"What?"
"You."

I can't take much more of this. It's been these same moments on repeat for weeks now. Ever since that stupid archangel Michael told me Ryan was dead, all I can think about and see is these moments with him. Moment's I'll never get to live again all because they saved the wrong person.

Yeah, that's right. They saved the wrong person. I should be the one that's dead, but no, because of me being this ball of light from Heaven or whatever, I'm the one left here and he's the one that's faded into nothingness.

The nightmares, I can't stop them anymore. For the first week after Gabriel brought me home and I did the whole *'fake it 'til you make it'* thing with Emma and school, I'd be able to eventually shut my brain off at night. All it took was a load of sleeping pills and Nyquil and I was out like a light, not waking or remembering anything I might have dreamed when I got up over ten hours later.

Now though, I can't escape them. Ryan, he's haunting me, I'm sure of it. He comes to me when I'm sleeping, he invades my senses when I'm in the classes we shared and no method of self-medicating helps. Nothing helps. I haven't slept right in weeks and I swear to god, the good thing I had going here, making people believe I was absolutely fine, it's cracking and my true nature is starting to show.

Why the hell am I still here? How did things go so tragically wrong? He was supposed to save me and then we were supposed to get out of this together. It should be us going to class together, laughing, holding hands, and getting to really know each other. Not me going alone, keeping my head down, ignoring the world around me and wishing I was dead.

I still don't believe what the angels told me. What even God appeared to tell me before Gabriel brought me back. I don't believe they did everything they could to save the man I was ready to die for. I mean come on, they're freaking angels for Christ's sakes. If they couldn't save someone from a fate that wasn't meant for them, then who the hell could?

The truth is they let him die because they hate him. He was part demon, which made him nothing to them. He could have been filled with more light than I have inside me and it wouldn't have made a damn bit of difference. They made up their mind a long time ago about Ryan McGregor and they're probably beyond happy he's dead.

I'm not happy though. I hate this. I hate the way I wake up screaming every morning because just the sound of his voice in my dream is enough to make my heart rip out of my chest all over again. I hate the way I can barely breathe all day as I go from one pointless class to the other. I'm barely hanging on and even if there was someone I could reach out to, beg to save me before I end up driving myself off the proverbial cliff, I wouldn't do it. I can't bring anyone into the mess that is my heart and mind. I can't let them see the darkness I'm living in.

The darkness I've been living in for weeks without him.

Emma; she can tell something's going on with me, but because I haven't said a word since I got back, she has no idea what it could be. I'm sure she can see that Ryan isn't in our classes anymore, so it won't take her long to figure out it's about him. The last she knew though, Ryan had run from me after our kiss so there's a small chance she won't even think about him at all. She hates him, probably as much as Heaven and that's my fault too.

I made her think he was a bad guy when in reality he was just holding on to something that would destroy me. He died looking out for me and what am I doing with the life he gave me back? Pissing it away because the wrong people lived and died that day. With him gone, Lucifer dead, there's nothing left for me to even bother caring about. I'm completely empty and numb.

I want to die.

If I would just grow a set and do away with myself, I might be able to end up where he is right now. We could be together, the way we should have been here and weren't able to. That want, the need to be with him, it's the only thing that keeps me moving every day. Hours turn into days and those days into weeks and I just hold onto the same notion that if everything just ended for me right now, I could finally have what I want most. I just can't bring myself to do anything about it and I hate myself even more.

He wasn't supposed to leave me. We didn't get to have our epic love story. The one that even Lucifer couldn't beat. God gave me a small taste of simple perfection and then he said *'nope sorry, you're not allowed anymore of that'* and ripped it all away from me while I wasn't even coherent enough to experience it. I wasn't even with him when he died. They took that away from me too.

I hate them. All of them. I never want to see them again. When Gabriel dropped me off and bathed me in his light, I didn't even feel it. I can tell that it upset him, but I didn't care then and I don't care now. All I felt was empty. If the light couldn't save the one person deserving of it, than I didn't want any part of it and I don't care how upset it makes them.

I think that's what's going on with me. When Ryan died, I died with him or at least the parts of me that were worth anything did. There's nothing left now but this body, a shell that I walk around in every day, going through the motions, waiting for the end to come. I feel like a zombie, the one you see in the movies and television, slumping along with only one goal in mind.

Theirs is to feed and mine is to appear like I'm golden. That I'm okay and not completely destroyed underneath it all.

People can think what they want about the way I'm acting. I don't give a shit. They can say that we weren't really in love, that what we experienced was just an intense lust for one another, an endorphin rush or whatever, but it's all bullshit. I felt real love, real acceptance and the very second I felt it, it was ripped from my grasp, leaving nothing but numbness behind.

Shit. It's happening again. I can feel him, like he's right here with me, his lips close to my ear and the small bit of air he's releasing from his nose as he breathes is tickling my hair, causing my body to shiver and shake with the sensations it stirs in me.

"Well let me tell you a little secret. You only think I'm staring at Suzy and in a way I suppose I am, but it's not intentional."

"Oh really? Then what exactly is it that you're doing, McGregor?"

"Watching you, Richards. Happy now?"

Someone needs to put me out of my misery. I can't take much more of this. His voice is still like music to my ears. Maybe even more so because I know he's never coming back. Whatever the reason for these haunting memories doesn't matter, I just want them gone.

If he had just stayed away from me, realized that he was changing sides and backed off, leaving me alone or even making Lucifer deal with me, he might be here now. He wouldn't have been ripped away the way someone rips off an old Band-Aid and he would still get to enjoy his life.

I know he hasn't exactly had an amazing life, but anything had to be better than just being gone forever.

Michael says he's in Purgatory, that because he isn't quite human or demon, he would have ended up there instead of just ceasing to exist and I suppose that should make me feel better but it doesn't. He shouldn't be anywhere but right here on this campus, doing what he was doing before he walked in and held out his hand that day in Psych class.

This is all my fucking fault.

Serenity, you must stop thinking that way. It is not true.

Great. So not only do I get to deal with Ryan's voice in my head, his scent, his heart-stopping stare, but now I've gotta deal with an archangel too? No way. I'm not in the mood for this right now.

"Go away, Gabe."

I think I have been away long enough.

Can't argue with him on that. He hasn't spoken to me or appeared in weeks. I guess when your final words are that you wish he would screw off and die, it doesn't inspire him to wanna come around. I meant what I said though, I want him gone. Dead wouldn't be so bad either.

I am sorry that I cannot accommodate that particular wish for you.

"What do you want?"

Doesn't he understand that being here is just making everything worse? Of course he does. He can read my thoughts. He knows what being here is doing to me, the shit it brings up and as is the angel way, he doesn't care. Well, I'll show him a thing or two about someone not caring because I definitely don't care why he's here or even what he's going to say next.

I want what I have always wanted as it pertains to you, Serenity.

Great. He wants my heart.

That is not what I mean and if you reach inside yourself, you know that.

"Well I'm sorry, but whatever it is you want from me, I can't give you. I've got nothing left to give or haven't you figured that out yet?"

You still have a lot that you can give both me and the world around you. Right now you are just lost in the grief you feel. It will pass.

Easy for him to say. He didn't lose the other half of his heart.

Yes I have. Do not tell me that I do not understand your loss because as sure I am speaking with you now, I have felt the loss of the other half of me.

I need to get out of here. Shit. I know what he means and it's gonna make the waterworks start. I can't break down, not again. I've been crying nonstop for weeks, I need a break from it. I can't let this angel bring it all back. No way, no how.

I am sorry Serenity. It was not my intent to come here and cause you more upset.

"Just tell me what you want."

I hate the quiver in my voice, the way it shakes and cracks. It's a dead giveaway that I'm not alright. Truth is, I hate every sound I make. I can't stand any of them. I just wanna rip my vocal chords out so I never have to make another sound again.

I do not want anything but for you to feel okay again. I am here now for that reason alone. I cannot let you go through this alone anymore. I tried, but it would appear as though I suck at it.

"You—suck at it?" I repeat, shocked to hear him sounding human for the first time since I've known him. Have things really changed that much since I checked out and he's doing what I wanted him too all along?

It would seem as though you have worn off on me. Do not get used to it, I am not sure how I feel about it.

"Yeah I'm not so sure I like it all that much either."

We're off topic now, his attempt at distracting me working for once. It's the first time in weeks that I haven't experienced the sound of Ryan's voice every waking second. It feels good but the minute I admit that, I feel sick. I shouldn't be feeling good at all with everything that happened. I deserve misery.

You deserve nothing of the sort, Serenity. It is perfectly acceptable for you to feel something other than hatred for yourself. Do you believe Ryan would want this for you?

No, he wouldn't want me doing this, but since he's not exactly here to argue with me, it doesn't matter what he wants now. I'm the one left here to pick up the pieces and I'll do it any damn way I feel like.

"Can we not do this? I need to get to class. Gotta keep up appearances."

Do whatever you feel you need to, but Serenity do not hesitate to call for me if it becomes too much. I have stayed away because I wanted to give you time, but I am back now and I will never leave you again.

I can tell by the silence in my mind that he's gone, the familiar buzz that blankets my mind whenever he's near and speaking completely gone and the numbness returning in waves. It's feeling the emptiness again that I want to call out for him, but I keep my mouth firmly shut. I can't depend on him to help me with this.

Depending on someone, leaning on them to help with the agony I'm feeling would only wind up hurting more in the long run than it does right now. Attachment of any kind does nothing but cause pain because in the end it can be taken away just as quickly as it's given.

It's true what they say. Everybody does leave.

Gabriel

It is far worse than I thought. Not only is Heaven's ball of light drowning in her own grief and loss, but she is also fighting the urge to end her very existence. With the path she finds herself on, it is only a matter of time before Father becomes involved and sends down a bringer of light to handle the situation.

I cannot let that happen. Serenity is not just another human near her breaking point. She is not destined for the darkness and in need of rescue. Even if she were, it would be up to me to save her. Me and no one else. It is what a guardian angel does. It is also what I would gladly do as her beloved, but just like in times past, I cannot let our bond be the guiding force.

I have to allow her to come to me in her own way and pray that she does so before it is too late and she does the unthinkable.

Graham has returned to school and just as he stated during our brief conversation a few short weeks ago, he is watching over her, biding his time until he can make his entrance. Where I have no doubt he is being guided by his own bond the way that I am, he is fighting it because he wants to do much the same as I do. He wants to handle Serenity in the right way.

There was a time not that long ago where I was willing to stand before the half demon and fight in order to keep these two apart, but with everything that has happened since, what I have learned of Lucifer and his manipulation of me, I can see now how wrong I was.

As badly as I want Serenity to be with me, I know that it is not possible. She will be mine in her own time and I have to accept that, which means accepting whatever is to happen next, especially what happens with the soul-mate.

It is difficult for me, entering her mind now that our bond has been activated. It pains me not to reach out and bring her close to me, protecting her from everything that she is facing. The same heart wrenching agony she feels, I am experiencing, but magnified. It is so intense that it is a wonder I am able to continue moving at all.

Graham needs to make his move. I have reached out in the only way I can, despite what it causes me to do so. It's up to him now. She needs to know that she is not alone and it has to come from as many of us as possible. It is becoming so important, this mission to bring the broken angel back to us that I have flirted with the idea of telling her friend.

Emma Daniels has been a guardian before and I know that if needed, she very well could be again. She has accepted Serenity and her differences in a way that no one before her has and it is that acceptance, that deep intensifying love that I know would aide in bringing her back to us. To where she needs to be.

Do not think about meddling in affairs that you have no business being in, brother. If Emma Daniels is to know the truth than Father will be the one to handle it.

"Taking a walk around in my mind Michael? Were you not the one that told me that you loathed when it happened to you? Do you not think it works the same way for everyone else?"

You are on a college campus, currently surrounded by more than one human. The last thing I want to do is read your thoughts, but it is not as if I can just appear before you and ask what is on your mind.

I cannot argue with him. I may be shrouded from them, but if Michael did appear there would be a shift in time and right now, wanting to stay under the radar, it is the last thing that needs to happen.

"Something needs to be done, Michael. She is near the end of her rope. We must rally as many people as possible to make sure that does not happen."

Trust in the Hudson boy. Let him attempt to break through. If that does not pan out the way that we hope then we will take our concerns to Father.

Of course Michael is the voice of reason. He is the one that thinks clearly in any situation and is able to see past the emotion. Where I want to jump in and save the day, for multiple reasons, he does not. He wants what is best for the ball of light, I have no doubt, but he wants to make sure that every avenue is tried before resorting to something that could twist the natural order of things.

"As you wish. I will stand down and allow Graham the chance to break through, but if it does not work out, I will waste no time taking this to Father. Emma Daniels needs to be told the truth, even if you do not see it."

All in due time, Gabriel. We will not let your beloved perish, remember that.

As the conversation ends, Michael pulling himself from my mind and again leaving me in peace, I think over all he has said. I know that Heaven will not allow anything to happen to Serenity, just as I would not, but I cannot help feeling that if she did give in to what she's feeling she would end up at home again, where things would be easier to manage.

She would revert back into what Father created her to be and all memory of Ryan McGregor and the loss suffered at his passing would cease to exist. She could be happy again and there is nothing more important to me than my beloved enjoying the happiness she deserves.

I would gladly lay down my own life to make it happen. Something that if what I am experiencing now as I make my way from the campus, is any indication, may indeed come a lot sooner than I think.

Chapter Four

Things Are Not As They Appear

Lucifer

Damn Gabriel and his ability to sense darkness.

When I made my way to the campus, it was to observe all that has happened in my absence. I had been able to catch a mere glimpse of the heavenly sacrifice, Serenity, but any more than that was impossible with Gabriel arriving on the scene not long after I did.

I am not sure why I am so put off by this occurrence considering that it is not yet time for me to make my presence known, but it is most unsettling. Commanding the level of power that I do, should have kept me cloaked from him. It appears as though the injury I sustained in our battle had caused more damage than I thought.

The angel blade turned out to be more than a prop after all. A shame really. If I had known that going into the battle, I could have done more damage than I did. There is no point in thinking about that now though as there is much that needs to be done.

They all believe me to have perished and for weeks now I have given them no reason to doubt it. I have managed to make my way out into the world in an effort to feed the way I am accustomed to without so much as a peep from the other side. If they are aware of my existence, they are not focusing on it the way they should be, which means that until such time as I am ready to stand before them all again, I can continue on as I have been.

What Serenity is experiencing is interesting to me. During one of my visits I was able to see that she is indeed coming apart at the seams. The loss of Ryan weighs heavily on her, far more so than I expected. When I realized what was taking place between them, the connection they seemed to share, it was new to me. A being of light and one as inherently dark as Ryan could just never exist together and they had proven me wrong. They continue to prove me wrong as evidenced by the way Serenity can barely breathe on her own, much less function.

I definitely need to look more into this connection. Doing so can only bring about a more positive result for me with what has to happen next. I have a surprise in store for the ball light and one that she will most definitely not see coming. It may not appear in the way that she wants it, but with the way she feels, I am sure she will eventually come to embrace it.

She will come to embrace me and the future we are destined to share together.

I will bide my time, plotting and planning even more so than I did the first time around, and when the time is right, I will make my entrance. The only difference between then and now is, this time I will not fail.

Serenity Richards will be mine and there is nothing Heaven can do about it.

Serenity

This class. I don't even know why I'm still in it. It's been proven that when I'm here the visions are worse than they are anywhere else. I see him in the seat across from me and for some sick reason I can't figure out, I refuse to leave the class or even change seats.

I'm starting to think I get some strange sense of pleasure from staying here. Like a big screw you to the angels and everyone around me that sees I'm not quite right. Even the teacher throws me these sympathetic looks because he knows that we got close before all hell broke loose. Yet I still sit here every single day going through the motions, my eyes trained on the doors like Ryan is going to walk back through them.

If I was smart, I would bring all of this to my teacher. I mean with as out of control as I've been feeling since Ryan died, who knows what I could turn into if left to my own devices. If I brought it to the professor, maybe he could steer me off this path and he wouldn't have an empty future serial killer in his midst.

Dramatic I know, but true. Underneath all the grief and loss I feel, there's anger there and eventually, if it just sits inside me, it's going to fester and grow so big that I'm not going to be able to control it anymore. I will snap and when I do, I can't promise anyone will be safe. Right now the only one I want to hurt is myself because it's my fault any of this is happening, but I also want to hurt the person that put this in motion in the first place.

God.

I want to kill God. It's his fault just as much as it's mine that Ryan isn't here. If he had seen the light inside the half demon when I did, he would have been redeemed sooner and none of this pointless shit would be happening right now. He deserves to burn as much as I do.

I can't think like this. Yeah, he's to blame, but the fire, burning, wanting him to pay, that's not me. It's Lucifer and it's exactly what we all fought so hard against in the first place. I would still choose the same way if all of this was repeated. Lucifer needed to be stopped even if it did take away the one person I felt something more than awkwardness for.

"What?"

"Oh it's nothing. I'm just really glad I didn't stay home today."

Things were so strange that first day. I went to class like normal, not at all surprised that Emma didn't show, her hatred for the class not exactly a state secret. I busied myself listening to the professor drone on about what we would be covering over the course of the next few months, all the while trying to put the horrible run-in I had with Gabriel from my mind.

Then in walks my best friend, but she's not alone. She's with the rock star. Before he told me the truth, in one of the times we hung out and the conversation hadn't turned to our abilities or the kiss we shared, I told him he looked like Jared Leto and he laughed about it. I think during those first few days together, that might have been the one thing I said that wasn't completely awkward.

Watching all the movies with Emma paid off and with the way the voices used to talk to me when he was around, it was obvious that I wasn't the only one who thought he looked like the guy. I'll never know now, but I'm pretty sure he thought I was crazy when I mentioned it. I'm also pretty sure Emma was proud of me for it, since doing it meant that I actually noticed guys other than Graham Hudson after all.

There's another situation that completely blew to shit. My relationship with Graham.

When I moved away from Green Haven, I never thought I'd see him again. It hurt, leaving him and moving on to a life that didn't have him in it, but it needed to be done. For two years I lived a life without him until one day he was here.

The fear I felt seeing him again, I can still feel it in my bones. It was the first time I ever felt anything remotely frightening with him, but that day, I couldn't get away fast enough.

I can't think about Graham. He's still out there somewhere. Ryan's not.

I need to think about him though. He's the only thing this morning that's been able to block my memories of Ryan and if I plan on making it through this class without breaking down in front of everyone, I need as much of that as I can get.

It took him two years, but he finally told me the truth about what happened before I moved away. What our kiss meant. There was this second when he was telling me everything where my heart softened and I wanted the exact same things as him.

Graham and I, we've always had this comfortable way with each other and when he put everything on the line, it's like the dam broke and the distance of the last two years, the fact that we hadn't spoken once in all that time, it was forgotten and we were right back in Green Haven all over again and he was my best friend and first love.

It's selfish, but I could really use some of that now. I could use Graham. I'm not naïve enough to think that he can take what I'm feeling away, but I don't think he can make it worse. I need to feel comfortable again because I'm not sure how much more of this I can take.

The sound of a throat clearing jolts me and despite knowing that it's a long shot, my eyes dart straight over to the vacant seat beside me, expecting to see those blue eyes staring back at me, the smirk firmly in place, as if nothing that happened weeks ago was real.

It's too good to be true because just like always, the seat is as empty as I am and it takes everything in me to keep my breathing level and not crack under the weight of the truth. It's only when the voice clears again and a shadow moves over my desk that I finally avert my gaze from his seat and look up, coming in contact with the last person I expected to see.

"Fancy meeting you here."

Graham

When I saw her again, spoke to her the first time, I knew it wasn't going to be easy. I expected her to be stunned, especially with the class I'm throwing myself into, one that in a million years I would never be caught dead in. I definitely didn't expect this.

She's scowling at me. Serenity Richards, the girl I haven't been able to let go of, the one that haunts my dreams, gives me a constant what if, is actually sitting in her seat, her body rigid and she's scowling.

"Graham?" she whispers as her eyes look over to the chair to the left. "What are you—doing here?"

It's been a few weeks since she stammered like this. If I'm honest about it, it's been years since she's done it, at least the way she is now. She's the girl I remember, yet she's not. I can see the emptiness in her eyes and I can also see the fear.

She thinks I'm gonna sit in that seat, the one that I know is reserved for one person only. In order for me to come back and make it look like I'm not doing it in an effort to save her, I had to have as much info as possible and Gabriel had come through with it big time. I know Ryan sat there when he first appeared and every day they were together after and there is no way I'm stepping into the middle of that.

I won't take those memories away from her. I hate admitting it, but the demon opened her up in ways she hadn't allowed herself to since that night back home when she kissed me so recklessly. Taking away her time with Ryan, trying to force her not to focus on it would be wrong and I'm determined not to do things wrong anymore.

This time I'm going to get through to her the right way.

"Wanted to see what all the fuss was about."

Sliding into the seat behind her, another seat that I know belongs to someone other than me, I resist the urge to tap her on the shoulder and continue talking. It's another step I'm taking in an effort to feel her out and take my time. Moving too fast will only make her pull more into herself and that's not what I'm here to do. I'm here to make her live again.

Her body turns slightly, her head dipped backward toward me and the corner of her mouth lifts. At first I think she's smiling at me, her new version of a smile anyway, but that gets quickly thrown out the window as she gets right to business.

"Gabriel put you up to this, didn't he?"

"No."

I know it's a half truth, but right now, I can tell she's on guard which means I'm not the only one that's made an appearance recently. I'm not sure if I should be pissed or happy that he seems to have come back into her life instead of just watching from the sidelines the way he admitted to.

"Swimming in bullshit here, Graham Cracker."

"He didn't set this up. I swear to you. I'm here because I want to be."

"You wanna be in Psychology? Since when?"

"Since I found out that angels and demons are real and the devil wanted to marry you."

She flinches at my words and I swear if I could lift my leg up in this seat right now, I'd kick my own ass. Bringing up the night of the wedding isn't going to gain me any points with her, if anything it's going to make me lose her more. I should've known better.

"Sorry..."

"No, I'm sorry. You've got every right to be here. It just seemed strange."

"I take it Gabriel came by for a chat recently?" I ask, pushing her, wanting her to tell me things again.

"Yeah he did."

"He's worried about you."

This seems to spark something in her as her eyes rise in surprise.

"He's been to see you too?"

"Yeah, but I figure you had to see that coming, princess. If he can't get through to you, he's gonna bring it to me."

"At least he didn't possess you this time."

"Thank god for that."

The air goes dead around us and I'm confused. It seemed like I was getting somewhere and now all I can hear is the professor, his chalk hitting the board in front of him, squealing across as he writes something out that I'm pretty sure I'm gonna need to know if I'm staying in the class.

Thing is, I'm more concerned with her and why she's now turning back to the front of the room than I am with whatever happens in the class, so I press ahead even though I know I'm probably going to make it worse.

"What did I say?"

"I can't thank god for anything anymore."

Yeah, she's pretty far gone, no doubt about that now. Taking a figure of speech literally is not her style, especially with me. She never reads too much into things with me unless I'm giving her a reason to.

"Ser, I know it doesn't seem like it, but there's actually something you can thank him for."

Her body turns in toward me again and the joy I get from that one simple movement, it's crazy. I might be able to save this moment after all.

"Oh yeah, what's that?"

It would be so easy to tell her that she can thank god for her life, the reason she's even here at all considering that Heaven had done everything in its power to make sure that she wasn't lost, but I don't go there. I can't. That wound is fresh and it's the reason I'm here to begin with. So instead, I go with something far more selfish.

"You can thank him for me. Now you won't have to go through this shitty ass class alone."

Chapter Five

A Vision of Things to Come

Gabriel

With Graham making contact, I knew it was only a matter of time before I was called back home and when Michael sent word, I was ready.

Father has not been himself since the events in Green Haven and it is easy to see why that is. He is all knowing, there is nothing that he is not aware of, but according to him during the talks we have had together, Ryan's passing was unexpected. He was not slated to perish in the church.

I am not sure how something of that nature could have gotten past my father, but I know enough not to question him about it. If there is something he believes I need to know then he will tell me in his own time and not a second before. It would do nothing to push him to speak of it now. We are all on edge as it is.

When Serenity was created, she was made of the purest light. It was the very light that Father used to create Heaven and what had originally gone into his plan for the world and the humans that would inhabit it. There was no darkness surrounding it, it was always bright and happy, all of which Serenity is not anymore.

This is what causes Father the most concern. How twisted she has become in such a short period of time. He is struggling to find the parts of the light within her, which is why I stepped forward and went to Graham in the first place. If she is so far gone already that even my father cannot reach the parts of her that he put there in her creation, then there was only option left to pursue.

We would need to use the soul-mate bond even though Graham wants no part of it and bring her back where she belongs. Lucifer may have been defeated and the darkness banished for the time being, but that did not mean it was gone forever.

I am of the belief that it is not the loss she feels, the blame she is putting on herself that is turning her this way. I believe that there is more to it than that, but getting Father or even Michael to believe in it, has become increasingly more difficult.

Ryan and Serenity were connected during their brief time together. It stands to reason that because of that connection, the one that Heaven or Hell cannot quite make sense of, they would take on parts of each other. I believe that Serenity losing Ryan became more like him than was ever intended.

I also believe that if Ryan had survived, we would be seeing much the same inside of him. Serenity had seen it before she married him, the light that surrounded him, which leads me to believe that he was already going through changes. The issue I face is making my very set in their ways father and brother see it the same way.

A being of darkness and one of light cannot connect. We have been hearing that since the beginning of time. It is just not possible. I do think it is time for the rulebook, the way things have been to be rewritten because Serenity and Ryan are proving that they are not following the mold previously set. They are making one of their own even though he is no longer here to do it.

"You are still going on with that ridiculous notion of yours, Gabriel? When are you going to learn that what Father says is fact?"

"When you open your eyes and accept that maybe there might be some truth in what I am saying. You are able to witness her changes as easily as I am, Michael. She is not the Serenity he created. She hasn't been for some time now."

"I cannot argue that, but the explanation is simple. Humans, they do not deal with loss the way a celestial might. We are able to compartmentalize, put it away in such a way that it does not change who and what we are. They are unable to do the same."

"Is that what you did when you faced losing your beloved? Did you compartmentalize?"

"Faith has nothing to do with this and I urge you to remember that."

"She has everything to do with this. She could very well have been the one down there going through this. So before you completely discount all that I am saying, you might want to step into my shoes for a while, Michael. It is not as black and white as you make it out to be."

I rather enjoy the moments where he has no comeback for me. They are few and far between but when they do occur, I find happiness like I have never known. If I want to get Michael to think, all I need to do is bring up Faith and what they experienced together and it seems to make him see things a different way.

It's not as though he will change his way of thinking entirely, but just that brief second where he focuses on there being another way because of the similarities between Faith and Serenity is all I need.

"You have made a valid point."

"I usually do."

"Come now, we will discuss this later. Father wishes to speak to you. It is a matter of great urgency and a situation that we need you to be fully aware of so that you can move forward accordingly when you head back down."

There is always a matter of great urgency here. For the last century or so, it has always pertained to my fallen brother Lucifer in some way, but with him out of the picture, I am unsure what it could be. I am already aware of Serenity being our top concern and have been doing all that I can in order to get through to her. There is not much else that I need to be made aware of.

"Things are not as they appear little brother, but I will let our father fill you in."

"So this is about Lucifer?"

"Yes."

"Has Father figured out how he was able to walk through the holy fire, or is he still determined to leave that for us?"

"This is bigger than that. All will be revealed soon. Come now. He is expecting us."

Within seconds we are standing before the Almighty and his light is shining, only this time, there is no welcoming smile to greet me the way there would have been in times past. It is quite obvious standing here now that he has much on his mind and it is causing his normal demeanor to change in ways I am most unaccustomed to.

"I am overjoyed that Graham has agreed to step in and help with Serenity and that he seems to be making headway."

"As am I, Father."

"Can he be trusted to guard over her should we need it?"

That is an odd question. Graham is human even though he is bathed in the light just as his soul-mate is, a direct link to what they have always been to one another if there ever was one. He is not a warrior the way we are, but I have no doubt if called upon he would do everything in his power to keep the ball of light protected and safe.

"Do you believe we are going to need him in that way? Is that why you have called me here?"

"No. I am merely questioning you about the boy. I am aware of what lies within him and how he feels about Serenity, but I need to know if he can handle it should it be tested."

"I believe that he can handle anything as it pertains to her."

"Good. That is what I was hoping to hear."

"Father, I mean no disrespect, but you do not seem like yourself. I know the losses we have suffered in recent weeks has not been easy but this feels like something more. Will you please tell me what is going on?"

"Gabriel, as Michael has already told you, things are not as they appear. There is a force the likes of which I have never seen that is making itself known. It is that which has me reaching out to you now."

"What kind of force are we talking about? Does this have anything to do with Lucifer?"

"It has everything to do with him because he is the force of which I speak of."

First he asks me about Graham and his willingness to stand and fight in an effort to protect and now he is telling me that the brother I believed to be dead is in fact alive and coming back for more? How long has this been going on and why am I only finding out about it now?

"Lucifer did not perish. He is very much alive and he is dangerously close to your charge as we speak. I am unable to pick up on the vessel he is using, only that he has occupied and discarded three of them since he made his presence known. I believe you know what this means."

"We need to guard ourselves against another attack."

"Yes, but even more than that we need to be sure we are clued in to everything that happens and are in constant communication until we are able to learn more."

"There is more you are not telling me."

When one speaks with him the way I am, we have to be prepared that there is much he is not telling us. For whatever reason, he decides how much information to tell us at any given time and while in the past that way of being has caused a lot of problems, it is a way that will never change. If he exposes too much to us and the way things have been written is changed, it could mean even more disaster than what has already occurred and it is not a chance he is willing to take.

"Do you believe he is going to make another play for Serenity and her light?"

"I do. What you do not know is that if he gets close enough, this time we might not be able to prevent it."

"What does that mean?"

"For some time now we have believed Lucifer's power to originate completely in darkness. He had taken that which he was left with when he fell and twisted it in order to create new and darker power. That is not the case at all. Your fallen brother has gotten his hands on old angelic power. Until now I have been the only one able to control it and that is where my concern lies. With this power he is unstoppable."

"Unstoppable? Father, you are the most powerful being in all of creation. Lucifer can be stopped, we just need to find the way to do it."

"No, Gabriel. As I have already told Michael, the one chance we had at finishing him once and for all because of the power he wields, died that day in Green Haven."

What does this have to do with Ryan? Does the son need to kill the father?

"No. Gabriel, it is time I told you everything, but be warned, you are not going to like what it is that I have to say and above all else, Serenity must never learn of it."

Serenity is my beloved. There is a connection between us that is unmatched. The moment it was ignited it opened us up to each other, as much as it can with her limited knowledge of it. It means that whatever Father wants me to keep from her, I am going to be unable to do. She will be able to read me to find out.

"She is unaware that she can read you, so that is not an issue. You must keep this which I am about to tell you to yourself Gabriel. It is a matter of life or death."

"Fine, I will keep it from her until such time as it becomes impossible to do so. What is this matter of life and death and how does it pertain to the half demon?"

There is a look that occurs between Michael and our father and as both of their expressions turn grave, I believe I already have the answer to my question. Ryan, the human demon hybrid is more than I first believed him to be. There is no other explanation.

"You are correct, Gabriel. Ryan is not a hybrid for the darkness the way he appeared. He was a pure angel."

"Excuse me?"

"Gabriel, you sound human right now. Do you wish for me to repeat Father's words back to you?" Michael says, his expression changed again, now displaying a crooked smile at my expense.

"Michael, now is not the time to be smart." Father admonishes before turning his attention back to me. "The one being in all of creation that is able to combat the old power, is the purest angel in Heaven. There were five in existence, but as you know, four of them had been lost in battle and the other one, ceased to exist."

"Then how is Ryan the pure angel?"

"He is the one that ceased to exist. The one that we could not track. Twenty-one years ago, a mistake was made here in Heaven and he was sent down in place of another light."

I cannot believe what I am hearing. Not only did Serenity see the light around him before his death, trying to get us to believe in her belief that he was good despite the lot he had been given, but he had also proven it himself by taking his own life in order for her to live on. That alone should have been enough guilt for all of Heaven to carry, but now there is so much more.

He was a brother and he died before any of us got the chance to fix the mistake.

"He was never meant to be a demon?"

"No."

"Heaven screwed up? We did this to him, you did this to him and now to your ball of light."

"Gabriel, you must remain calm and watch what you are saying."

"I am not going to do anything of the sort! You are both standing here telling me that Ryan was our brother, one of us and he got sent down by some angelic error, forced to live unspeakable horrors, which he then brought onto Serenity. The very light of Heaven that you took so much pride in!"

"I am aware of what happened Gabriel, there is no need to remind me."

"You see the way she is. The absolute heartbreak she is experiencing down there right now that not even her soul-mate can break through. All of that could have been prevented twenty-one years ago! This would not be happening if you had paid more attention to all that you claim to love."

I will pay for my words here today, I am aware, but right now I do not care. They want me to keep this from her and I do not think I can. She deserves to know that she was right all this time. What she saw in the boy was pure and true because Ryan was made of the light just as she was. I know what I promised them, but I cannot do it.

Serenity needs to know this, even if it causes me to burn.

"You will do nothing of the sort, Gabriel. This needs to remain between the three of us. If she is made aware and it somehow slips out, Lucifer could use it and destroy the very being you claim to love!" Father shouts, using my own words against me.

"I will not keep this from her. She believes herself to be the cause of his death. She thinks that she put him on this course when in reality, you did it by taking your attention away."

"Gabriel, you are dangerously close to crossing a line you will not be able to come back from."

"I no longer care. I will do what is needed to protect her to the best of my ability and keep Lucifer away from her when he does return, but I will not go along with this. Keeping secrets is tired and overdone. We need to do things differently or we're going to continue to make mistakes like we did with Ryan. I do not know about the two of you, but I do not want that on my conscience."

"You will not tell her this. I will bind you to home if that is what it takes."

"Do whatever you have to do. You always do anyway. Just know that I will find my way back to her and she will learn the truth, no matter what you do. It is the right thing to do."

Chapter Six

The Beat of My Broken Heart

Serenity

Well, I never thought I'd come back here again.

What started as a random drink in high school, Mom having run out of soda and me desperately needing something to get motivated enough to go to hell—school, I'd poured my first cup of coffee into a mug and the rest is history. When I left Green Haven for school, I made it a point to find every coffee shop in the radius so I was only steps away from my next fix.

My need for all things caffeinated changed the same as everything else did a few weeks ago. The last time I came here, I was with Graham, the same way I am now, but nothing about this particular visit feels right. I want to get up from the table and head back to my room, bury my head under the covers; not coming out again until tomorrow morning when the routine of my life starts over again.

Here I am, across from him, his eyes the same soft green they've always been whenever we've spent time together, but unlike the last time where I opened up and told him the truth about everything, this time all we're surrounded by is everyone else's noise and none of our own.

I can't open up to him. There's nothing left to say. I'm happy he's here, it's comforting even though I don't deserve it, but he knows everything now and the things I can't bring myself to say, I'm pretty sure Gabe has already filled him in on, so mute seems to be the way to be.

Memories, they're funny things. For weeks the only ones I've been able to conjure up in my mind, focus on so intently have been the ones with Ryan, but the minute Graham asked me to grab coffee with him even though I know he hates the stuff, there they were again only this time the stars changed.

Now I see what happened the last time, hear his words and despite feeling numb inside lately, reliving his angry tone, still has the ability to rip me apart from the inside out. His truth, the way he felt, I can't escape it. I really hate memories. I wish the angels wiped my mind when they had me in Heaven because right now, all this remembering—it's torture.

"He was right when he came to me. Even though he kept the truth from us, he was right. He wanted to protect you from the darkness, but at the time he couldn't figure out what that was. He came to me because he thought I'd be able to save you before you made a stupid mistake. Obviously we were both too late for that one."

As much as I hate remembering, running from them just makes it worse. Graham was right that day and I feel like I should tell him that. He needs to know that I get it now. They were too late to stop me from making a stupid decision. If I had just listened to him than maybe Ryan would still be out there somewhere.

"Don't do that, Ser Bear."

My nickname. The one I went two years without hearing and then the weeks again since. It's not the nickname that gets to me but everything else he's said.

"Don't do what?"

"You're frowning. I'm not an idiot. I know what you're doing. Where we are, it's bringing up old shit that's better off buried."

"How do you know that?"

"I know you, that's how."

"You're not reading my mind?"

He laughs and despite the seriousness of the conversation, I can feel my lips crack and rising at the sound. I'm gonna smile for the first time in what feels like forever and despite wanting to do it, I know I can't. I don't deserve to smile after everything that's happened.

"Does it look like I could read your mind? Ser, even if I had that power; girls, they don't make a whole lot of sense to me. It's like walking through a minefield."

"Ha-ha. Very funny." I answer, reaching across the table and slapping him, immediately pulling my hand back the minute I realize what I've done. I'm acting like I used to, pretending that things didn't change so drastically and I'm not mourning the loss of the man I married and loved.

"Serenity," he sighs. "You're allowed to do more than just go through the motions. You're allowed to live."

"No, I'm not."

"Who determines that? Who says that just because you're here and he isn't that you have to stop living, feeling and just perpetually go through the motions like a fucking robot all the time? Please tell me because I need to kick their ass."

Same old Graham. He never changes despite the hand he was dealt in the end. I walked into that conversation with him that day knowing he was in love with me, that he wanted me back and I didn't care. I still twisted the knife in his chest by admitting to my feelings for Ryan in an effort to be honest. I don't deserve him to be here like this right now, treating me the way he always has.

I deserve so much worse.

"I guess you need to kick my ass because I'm the one that can't do what you say I should."

"It can be arranged." He smirks at me before tipping the cup to his lips and draining it. "I've been dying to give you a spanking since the day I met you."

Damnit. I'm laughing. It was bad enough when it was the smile, but now I can actually hear the sound of my voice as I'm laughing at his crazy comment. I'm responding the way I always do with Graham and I don't know how I feel about it. The hole in my chest, the one that's been there since I found out about Ryan, its lighter somehow, closing in on itself a little. Him being here, taking my attention off everything, it's nice.

I don't want it to be nice. Letting this happen just proves what a horrible person I am.

Shit. Now I'm laughing so hard I'm crying. He's sliding his chair over to me, I can hear the scraping noise across the ground and see his shadow as it covers me. Damnit. No. This can't happen. He can't get close to me. Anytime anyone gets close to me they end up dead.

Graham can't die.

"Don't touch me."

He recoils at my words and the clipped tone, but he doesn't stop the way I want him to. No, he moves in as close as he can and now his arms, they're coming around me even though I'm sitting. His body is leaning across me. I can smell him, the familiar chocolate scent. God. I'm gonna throw up.

"Graham—"

"Ser, don't tell me not to hold you. Don't tell me that you don't need this. Don't sit here and tell me that you don't think you deserve this because fuck, you deserve so much more than this and I'm not gonna stop."

My body betrays me, sinking into his and that's when he slides his hands down lower and before I know it, I'm being lifted until I'm in his lap, his arms again coming to rest around me in a hug, holding me, protecting me like he's always done. Safely locked up in his cocoon.

He's not done though. Just when I think that holding me is going to be the worst of it, I feel his breath on my ear, which only causes my body to betray me more as it shivers, but it's not that reaction that gets me. It's what he says.

"When Mom told me she was sick; that she didn't have much time left, I swear to god Ser, I died right there in her room. It felt like I'd been ripped from my body completely. There was nothing worth living for if I had to face my life without her. I didn't want to live. I got up every day, went to school, painted, worked and then came home to do it all over again the next day. I get it."

I'm crying now, I can feel my body shaking under the force of the sobs coming from my throat, but I can't hear it. All I can hear are his words, the truth in them. He does get it. His mom is still alive, so he might not understand it entirely, but he gets the emptiness I feel. His hand strokes up and down my back but instead of soothing me the way I'm sure he intends, it just threatens to break me even more.

Graham shouldn't be the one touching me this way. It's reserved for Ryan.

"I just want—it to stop." I choke out. "I can't make it stop."

"Then let me." he whispers and I melt, sinking even more into him, his arms tightening their hold, never once wavering from me.

"I can't do—I can't bring you into this."

"Why not? Is there some rule that you have to go through this alone or that I can't help my best friend when she needs me the most?"

"No" I say the sound muffled from my place in his shirt. The shirt I've now made wet with my tears.

"So it's settled. You're not going through this alone anymore. I'm here Ser, and I'm not going anywhere."

"Even if you'd be safer staying as far away from me as you can get?"

"Even then. You're stuck with me, Ser Bear."

The way he says it, so positive, no conviction at all, I want to believe in it. He's extending me this olive branch, telling me that he's here for the duration and I want to grab on it and never let go because despite my need to do this on my own, to suffer in silence, I can't follow through. I need help.

I need him and I hate that I do because he's not Ryan. It's not fair that Graham is the runner-up. He should be the winner.

"If I asked you to take a road trip with me, would you do it?" he asks, bringing me away from the dark place my mind is threatening to go and back to reality.

"A road trip?"

"Yeah. It's stupid, but my mom's diagnosis, after I heard it I ran. I stole her car and I drove. It didn't make anything easier, but for a little while, I was able to get away from the reality of what I had coming for me. Maybe getting out of here can do the same for you, at least for a little while."

"It doesn't matter where I run Graham. He always finds me."

"Maybe so, but this time you've got something you didn't have before."

"What's that?"

"Me."

Graham

God I'm such an asshole. When I offered to take her for coffee, it was to get her away from that stupid routine of hers. I didn't want her going back to her room and hiding away for the night the way she's been doing. I wanted more.

Everything else, not what I wanted at all. It wasn't my intent to bring everything up the minute we got our drinks and sat down. It also wasn't intentional to bring her into my lap so I could hold her, but I did it and now I feel like an asshole because I'm enjoying it a little too much.

I've been dying to hold her like this for two years. Well, maybe not like this, the reason I'm doing it, but having my arms around her at all, rubbing her, feeling her skin, it's been two years in the making and even though I can tell she's struggling with what it means, I can't let her pull away.

This road trip idea, it's all true. I met Serenity after my mom had already been diagnosed and we were well on our way towards her inevitable end, so she doesn't know about any of this, but it all happened. Joey and me, we hotwired my mom's car and off we went. We weren't even legal to drive but the urge to get the hell outta town for a while, it drove me more than common sense did.

I want to do this for her. My time away from Green Haven, my mom's illness and all that was gonna come along with it, helped. I want to take her away from Stephenville, the memories she has here of her time with Ryan and I want to have her breathe in the air again, feel life around her. If it could help me and how messed up I was, I know it will do the same for her.

We're the same soul after all. Two separate parts but the same. What is good for me; my heart, it will be the same way for her and right now that's what drives me. This isn't about me and how tremendous she feels being in my arms again, it's about her and making sure that even for a few hours she sees another reason to stay.

Another reason to live.

I even know where I'm taking her. It's probably not the best idea in the world considering what happened the last time we were all there, but there's no better place than there for her right now.

Green Haven Memorial Park. The one place in the world that she could escape to when life with her mom got too hard. It was a place for her to feel safe, feel alive again even though she wanted to give up more than she wanted to keep fighting back then.

It won't be a short visit either. I want this to last longer than a couple of hours. She was always at her best at night, lying on the grass, looking up at the stars, sometimes even talking to them. When I caught her the first time after she told me about hearing voices, I assumed she was talking to ghosts; spirits of people that didn't want to pass on, but the more time I spent with her out there, I learned what it really was.

She had a connection with the sky; angels and Heaven then, even if we didn't know it at the time. Looking up at the stars, focusing on them, telling them all her secrets; that was her relief. That's exactly what she needs now. It's the one thing I'm positive will bring her back from the edge she's on.

"Where did you have in mind?"

"I can't tell you that. It's a surprise."

"You know I hate those."

"Exactly why I'm doing it. You're gonna hate me the entire drive, which frees your mind up from everything you've been dealing with. Once we get there though, you're gonna love me."

"Hate to love that quickly huh? This place must be epic."

"It is. You'll see."

"Can I tell you something?"

I nod and she smiles weakly, her cheeks rising but the light I'm used to seeing not there at all. Her eyes still cold and vacant, despite the casual tone.

"I'm not sure I should do this."

"Why?"

"When I'm here with the memories, hearing his voice in my head, seeing him so clearly, it's like we're still connected. If I leave with you right now and go away, even for a little while, I'm scared when I get back he won't be here anymore. I'll lose the connection."

Hearing her talk about Ryan like this, it hurts like a bitch, but I get what she's saying and I need to push past my own feelings. I can't be selfish now even though I want to be. I want to make her forget Ryan McGregor ever existed.

I want to remind her what we almost had. I don't though. I do the right thing even though I struggle through every second of it.

"The connection you two have, it doesn't go away because you do. It's always with you. Right here." I place my hand over her heart, her eyes instantly falling to the spot and rewarding me with a wistful smile. "No one can ever take him away as long as you keep him there."

Am I actually saying this shit right now? Where is it coming from? This is my girl for crying out loud. She's been mine since the day she moved in next door. I'm the only one that should be in her heart.

Graham I understand where you are coming from, but please do not take that path right now. You are doing a good thing here. Do not taint it.

Great. Gabriel.

I know why he's here now. I'm making this personal which is what I told him I wouldn't do. I need to get my head in check before I blow this before it starts.

"So will you do it? Take a road trip, just you, me and the open road?"

I hate that she seems so conflicted by such a simple thing. It would have been so easy to get her to do this two years ago. It's just proof that things have changed, not only for me but her too. She's never going to be the Serenity I knew again.

I don't want her to be the same. She's always been strong underneath her awkwardness and I noticed the change in her when Gabriel got me to come here the last time. That version of her, the one that spoke her mind, didn't let the angel walk all over her, that's the version of her that I want.

It's the version of her I'm determined to bring back.

"Okay Graham. Let's take a trip."

Chapter Seven

Present Everywhere

Serenity

Green Haven.

God, I hate this place. Why he chose to bring me here makes no sense. This is the last place I want to be right now. If there were memories I didn't want to relive in Stephenville, it's even worse here. This is the town of horrors. The place where the boy I fell in love with, wanted to save so badly lost his life in order to save mine.

Definitely not the happiest place on Earth.

I hate admitting it, but once Graham started driving, I closed my eyes and allowed sleep to take me. It's the first time in a long time where I closed my eyes and didn't wake up in a sweat over the nightmarish images that haunt me. It's probably the most peaceful sleep I've had since Gabriel used to come and sing me to sleep to keep the voices at bay.

The minute he pulls to a stop in the car and I wake up, seeing for myself where we are, I want to close my eyes and go right back where I was. I don't want to be here now. It might not be the exact place where everything happened, but it's still the town. I left this town for a reason two years ago. Lucifer brought me back here and again I'd been taken away. I didn't want to ever return.

Green Haven represents everything I've ever loved and everything I've lost. It's not just Ryan. It's the guy sitting across from me in the car right now too. He might be back in my life again, but I did lose him. For two years I went through the motions of my crazy life without him and that wound is still deep.

"You were wrong."

"Yeah I sort of figured I would be. You're pretty pissed at me right now, huh?"

"Pissed is an understatement. There's no word for what I feel right now."

"Ser, before you kick me out of the car and drive over me, will you hear me out?"

I've been thinking up a few good scenarios about what I wanted to do to Graham now that I know where he wanted to take me, but driving over him in his car wasn't one of them. Definitely gotta keep it in the list though, it's not half bad.

"You've got five minutes to explain this or I'm gonna get out and walk back to school."

"Eleventh grade. The big blow out with your mom, the one that had you running to my house in tears, wanting to run away and asking me to help you do it."

"What about it?"

"That's the reason I'm bringing you here. Do you remember what we did that night?"

"You talked me out of running away, said it would be smarter if we just hid out at the park for a while. We argued back and forth about it, because I was stubborn and thought you didn't wanna help me out. You grabbed me by the hand and dragged me all the way here."

"Right, but what else? What happened once we got here?"

"You started climbing trees and called me a baby because I wouldn't do it too?"

His laughter fills the car and it twists me up inside because just like at the coffee shop a few hours ago, it feels so good to hear him laughing like this. I like the rough sound of it. It's familiar.

"Yeah, that happened too, but what did you do? Come on princess. Don't make me spell it out for you. Something happened that night. You did something that even now I can't seem to forget even though I probably should."

"You're talking about me lying out here talking to the sky, aren't you?"

He nods and I blush. God, the way I was back then, so tied up in knots all the time, desperate to break away from the mother that didn't seem to give a shit if I lived or died. It was horrible. I did the strangest things. At first I kept them to myself, but eventually Graham and Emma both found out about it.

It's a time in my life I'd completely forgotten about. Not being here anymore meant that I didn't have to think about the past and for the longest time I liked it that way. I still like it that way. I don't wanna remember any of this.

"Lucifer brought me here. He tied me to that tree right over there." I point out the window and his eyes follow me until they lock right on the location I'm talking about. "He wanted to torture Ryan."

"Shit, Ser. I had no idea!" He slams his hands on the steering wheel and despite expecting it, I still jump. "I never would have brought you here if I knew that. I screwed this entire thing up."

He kind of did, but I'm not gonna tell him that because I get what he's trying to do. Not all of my time in Green Haven was bad. There were good memories, most of them surrounding him and he just wanted to give me that back. It's one of the reasons I loved him so much. He's just so innately good inside.

"No you didn't, Graham." Reaching across the car, I rest my hand on top of his and squeeze gently. The small initiation of contact, I expect the guilt to rise up but instead all I feel is my head start to spin. A reaction I've had forever with him and one that doesn't scare me near as much as it should. "Come on. You brought me here for a reason. It's time for you to get on with it."

His eyes catch mine and I offer a weak smile, this time feeling it more than I did back in Stephenville. A warmth comes over me when his lips rise and he returns my smile with one of his own. Whatever I felt when he showed up here, the urge to beat the hell out of him, it's gone now, replaced with something else entirely.

Safe. Comfortable. Protected. Okay.

For the first time in weeks, I actually feel okay and breaking away from him, I slide my hand off and slip myself out of the car as quickly as possible. I can't feel okay. I just can't. I also can't let him see just how much all of this is getting to me. He can't know he's the cause.

If he knows, it will change everything and I'll lose him again.

Graham

She jumps from the car so fast that it takes me a second to realize what happened. Once my brains starts functioning again though, it all makes perfect sense.

This was a stupid move.

Coming back here, seeing her again, attempting to save her from herself without bringing my personal feelings into it was an idiotic move. It's impossible not to do that when we've got this obvious connection between us. I'm the king of bonehead moves and this one proves it. For a whole day I've managed to fool myself into thinking I could do this the right way, staying detached, but whenever she's in direct contact with my body in any way, it all goes to shit.

I am in love with this girl. Hiding that in an effort to do right by her is only making it worse. She knows how I feel, I've never hidden it from her, at least not since I came back into her life a few weeks ago. She's aware of the bond between us. Pretending the way I have been, it's the reason she ran from the car because there can't be any pretending with us.

Ever.

The second she put her hand on mine, I lost all ability to think clearly. My head, it was hazy and it only started to clear the minute she released the hold and had taken off completely out of the car. I need to do the same now. I need to get the damn seatbelt off and follow her, show her the reason I brought her here and make her believe in it, but I'm stuck in place.

I don't get the soul-mate bond at all. I mean I get what it means in a bigger picture kind of way, but how we interact with each other, that's where things are tricky for me. I've always reacted this way with Serenity. Whenever we touch, my focus goes to crap, but the rest of me feels alive. I always just thought it was that way because of our history, the friendship we built and the feelings I let get in the way of it.

That's not it though. It's always been this damn connection calling the shots. I can't even be sure if what I feel for her is really me feeling it or if it's our souls melding together whenever we touch. I don't want to be controlled by anything, least of all a bond, but there's no mistaking what just happened in here and why she ran.

It's too much for her. What we share, she's betraying Ryan because despite her mind wanting it to be another way, she's reacting to me. We're breaking through her grief over him. I'm doing what I set out to do but it doesn't make me feel good. This is not the way I want to do things.

What you are experiencing, it is being guided by the bond, but that is all. When you are not touching her, you still worship the very ground she walks on, do you not?

"You gonna keep doing that in my mind or just appear so we can talk like normal people? Wait—never mind."

Completely disregarding what I said, the car lights up and I'm staring into the irises of a very annoyed looking angel.

"If she catches me here like this, it will ruin all you have accomplished thus far. Do you really want to risk that to have a conversation?"

"No, not when you put it like that, but man, you coming into my head like that, it's kind of crazy."

"Well I cannot very well let you go on believing the nonsense you are feeding yourself."

"Nonsense huh?"

"Yes Graham," he sighs. "What you believe, the hold the bond has over you, it's nonsense. None of it is true. Yes, the two of you share a very powerful connection but that developed before the two of you touched."

"But when we touch, it's the bond right?"

"In a manner of speaking yes. It is the kinetic energy between both souls reacting to one another, but that is all it is. Everything else is the both of you."

"The both of us?"

"Please spare me the disbelief, Graham. It does not please me to have to talk about this considering the bond I share with her. Yes, the both of you. Serenity, despite her pain is very much in love with you. She always will be."

"Because we're bonded."

"Everyone claims that angels are the stupid ones. They have obviously not spent enough time in your company. I will only say this one final time and then you are on your own."

"Say what?"

"What you and Serenity share has nothing at all to do with lifetimes together, bonds or any other supernatural intervention. It is something that will always be present because of the very human bond you two share. The two of you might move on, be with other people but the love you have for one another, it will never die."

"Alright, I get it. It's not the bond and I'm ripping into myself over nothing. Is that all you came down to tell me?"

"No. There is more. Serenity is in danger. I cannot say more right now, but please, whatever you do, keep her close to you and do whatever is needed to protect her. I will control all that I can from my location, but I cannot do it without you."

"What does that mean?"

"It means I have learned some things recently that lead me to believe she is not safe. That is all you need to know for now."

"I'll do whatever I have to Gabe. You know that."

"Yes, you are right. I do."

"Is that why you seem upset? You're worried about her?"

He bows his head and sighs and something tells me with the way he's reacting that this is about a lot more than just being concerned for Serenity's well-being.

"I am worried about all of us. The war is not over, Graham. Now I must go. I have said far more than I should. Keep your guard up, please."

He's gone before I can answer and as I go over everything he told me, my eyes fall on the vision outside of the car. The girl that is now comfortably sitting under the tree I climbed one of the last times I brought her here.

Gabriel didn't have to ask me to watch out for her, keep her safe. I would do that regardless of the danger he spoke of. It's the one thing that in the last five years I've known beyond a shadow of a doubt that I'm good at.

It's also the one thing I would go to my death doing. Serenity would never be hurt again. Not as long as I'm breathing.

Chapter Eight

Bring You Home Again

Gabriel

"Just what is it that you are hoping to accomplish with that stunt you just pulled?"

Father's threat of keeping me in Heaven was an idle one and the second I had been able to get free of both him and Michael, I had taken it. I am pushing the envelope, I know but I meant what I said to them. Serenity and Graham deserve to know everything.

We kept things from her weeks ago and the end result while at first seeming to be a positive one, turned out to be anything but. The time for holding back with the ball of light was over. She deserved to know everything just as the rest of us did and nothing my brother will say to me now can change my mind.

"I did not set out to accomplish anything, Michael. I merely wanted to level the playing field, something I thought you would understand given your warrior origins."

"Where in what I asked you did you hear me say I did not understand?"

"Are you telling me that you do in fact get what I am trying to do?"

"Yes, Gabriel. Despite what you believe about me, we have been through enough during our time together where I am clued in to what guides you."

It should bring me solace, hearing him say that he understands what I feel I must do, but it does not. I need more than just his understanding. I want his acceptance and willingness to help me.

"You have it Gabriel. You have always had it. All you had to do was ask."

"Excuse me if I have a hard time believing that." I force a laugh. "With your position beside Father, you are the last person that would help me. Uriel is a better option and you know how he feels about the humans."

"Uriel prefers breaking magic and code. I prefer the fight. You know this."

"There is no fight, Michael. All we know is that Lucifer did not perish the way we first believed."

"But there will be a fight little brother, and when there is, would you not feel better having me on your side?"

There is no better warrior than Michael. He is the one you want on your side, no matter what you face, but in this case, not knowing what truly motivates him, I would rather go it alone then put my trust into the wrong being, even one as strong as my brother.

"Gabriel, I am going to spell this out for you the same way you did for Graham a few seconds ago. I want you to tell Serenity the truth. If Lucifer is back and making a play for her, she needs to know everything. I also believe that Graham should be informed as well. I am unsure why, but I see something in that boy."

"A little of yourself perhaps?"

"Could be. Whatever it is, they need to be informed, but if you are going to do it, we need to keep Father away from it for as long as possible."

"What are you suggesting Michael?"

This is not right. No one is more loyal to our father than Michael. He would lay down and accept defeat, going to his true death for our creator. What he is suggesting now, even though he has yet to give me the details, it is not like him at all. Surely he must realize what he is going to cause even suggesting this.

"I am aware of the consequences Gabriel. There was a time that I walked away from our father and Heaven as a whole for what I believed in. I am not afraid to do it again."

"How do you suggest we handle this?" I ask, choosing to disregard his step into my mind in favor of getting answers. "You see them now, are you sure this is the right moment to bring this to them?"

"I am not a firm believer in waiting with something of this magnitude. The sooner they know, the sooner we can deal with the fallout, whatever it may be."

There would be fallout. Serenity learning that the man she loved went to his death without the true knowledge of his creation would be enough to send her into an even more horrific downward spiral. Graham for all of his strength and light might not be enough to bring her back from this. I am no longer thinking of her as my beloved, but as the very real human she is.

This will destroy her, of that I have no doubt.

"We will give them the day, but by morning light this needs to be handled. I will figure out how we hide this from Father. I do have experience. You just make sure nothing happens in the meantime."

I am aware of what he means. I am to make sure no harm comes to her or Graham and keep Lucifer at bay should he choose this to be the time to make his grand entrance.

"I will do whatever is necessary, Michael."

"There is one more thing I want to discuss with you before I take my leave."

"The floor is all yours."

"I need to know where you stand." He pauses before again locking eyes with me. "There is a very good possibility that Lucifer returning this way has something to do with the undertaking. Serenity has to be the one to end his reign which means Father's end has not yet been reached. If we are to reach that point, where do you stand on what will take place next?"

Serenity was created for the sole purpose of ending the darkness forever. If she is to go up against Lucifer again and defeat him the way she had been unable to a few weeks ago, where I stand is clear. I am standing beside her always. This is not what Michael inquires about though. He is going far deeper with his concern. He is worried about what happens after everything has been completed and he has every right to be.

"She will make her way home. Are you ready to experience the beloved bond firsthand?"

"I do believe I was ready for it before it happened to you. If memory serves, you were the one that said the being slated for you would do better with me. You know how I feel about this, so the question does not even need to be posed."

"It does, Gabriel. This bond, it may have taken me quite some time to adapt to what it creates between the two beings it effects, but now that I have, I feel that I need to warn you. The way Serenity appears here, she will not be the same when she reaches Heaven."

"Is this where you tell me that she will be more like you? I am aware of that. I will accept her in whatever form she is given to me. It has been that way since the moment Father dispatched me on this mission to begin with."

"There is more."

"What more can there be? Have we not discussed this to death already?"

"The soul-mate, Gabriel. Surely you have given this some thought."

What does Michael know about Graham that I do not? Has Father given him some information as it pertains to the two of them that he did not believe I needed to be made aware of?

"No, this is not from Father, at least not entirely. This is just what I know. I promised her a long life at one point because Lucifer was supposed to have perished. Father told me that he wanted her to enjoy her human life before he brought her home. It does not appear to be that way anymore, but with her also comes her other half."

"Graham will be going home with her?"

"In a sense. Gabriel, they are slated to be joined back together. Serenity and Graham will become one again."

Chapter Nine

Ties That Bind

Serenity

Graham is crazy.

When he finally got out of the car and made his way over to where I was sitting under the tree, the last thing I expected him to do was lift his leg up over my head and attempt to climb the tree again the way he did a little over five years ago.

I admit, the minute I saw his leg rise, I thought for sure he was going to end up kicking me with it. Not intentionally of course, I saw he was going for the tree, but there was no real stop in between him jogging up to me and his leg going into the air. One small movement to the left or right and he would have hit me. Hard.

His laughter the minute I flinch is like music to my ears. The last few weeks, the haze I've been in, there hasn't been any laughter at all, not even from my best friend Emma and there's not many times where she's not cheery. I suppose that's what happens when you shut down on your best friend. She shuts down too. We haven't even spoken much lately, let alone laughed about anything.

A part of me misses that more than anything, but the other part, the one that knows I'm to blame for what happened won't let me do anything about it. If I go back to sitting around with her in bed, portable DVD player in hand watching chick flicks, it's time taken away from wallowing in my own hatred and that's not allowed.

Being normal has never been in the cards for me. There's no sense in starting now, even if that basic thing is as normal as my life has been since the day I started hearing voices in my head.

Graham climbing the tree though, it's like we're sixteen all over again and he's attempting to impress me by doing something that could easily get him hurt. It's like the first time he climbed the tree, all those years ago. The same level of fear is present for me, right along with the flakes of tree bark that are kicked off by his incessant climbing tactics.

"Isn't there an easier way for you to do that?" I call up and even though he's at least five feet higher than me now, I can still see the glow in his eyes and the smirk on his face.

"Princess Serenity doesn't like the bark in her hair?"

"More like I don't like the sap from the bark."

"I think it gives your hair a nice shine." He calls, his laughter falling down after his words and I can't help the short crisp laugh that comes out of my own mouth. It's hard not to do this with him. Even when I was at my worst, he still managed to bring it out of me. I'm just now sure how great I feel about it happening now.

"Yeah, you said that when the bird crapped in my hair too!"

"Cheap hair dye, Ser!"

There it is again, my laughter. The foreign sound I haven't heard in weeks. Before I get the chance to analyze it, I feel the ground shake and look up just in time to see Graham catch himself as he touches the ground.

"Didn't want to stay up there longer, monkey boy?"

"Just wanted to prove to myself I could still do it." He beams at me. "Still got it baby!"

"Yeah, yeah. You still got something alright."

He slides in beside me and leans his back up against the trunk. The way he's sitting, it reminds of the one time Ryan and I sat together on campus, when he told me that he prayed for me. Shaking it off, not wanting Graham to suspect where my mind is going, I paste on a smile and hope it's enough.

"You're thinking about him aren't you?" he whispers, rubbing his hand over my shoulder gently, igniting me. It's the same reaction I had in the car when I reached out to him.

Whenever we're in direct contact, it starts something I don't think I'll ever be ready to finish.

"That obvious?"

"Kind of. You get this look in your eyes, like you're someplace far away. Since it beats seeing your eyes showing nothing at all, I'll take it. What are you remembering?"

"When you sat down, the way you rested against the trunk, he did the same thing once."

"Ah, okay."

"I'm sorry." I apologize, feeling like shit for comparing the two of them. If it's wrong for me to even be here with Graham right now, it's even worse to find them similar. I'm betraying them both now instead of just one.

"Ser, you don't need to be sorry. I said some pretty horrible shit to you that day, ya know. I didn't understand what you were feeling and I was so damn jealous I couldn't even see straight. It's different now. I get it."

"You—do?" I stammer, unable to believe that his opinions changed all that much in the short time we've been apart.

"Yeah. You loved him and as hard as that is for me to accept, I do understand it. What he did for you, so you could stay, it's pretty fucking big. He's not at all what I thought he was. I'm the one that needs to be saying sorry."

I feel like somewhere in the world, hell is freezing over right now. Graham sitting here so casually and telling me that he's sorry for the things he said, for judging Ryan so harshly, it's unreal. I feel like I'm still back in the car asleep and this is the dream I've been stuck with.

"It's in the past."

"No it's not. Not really. As long as you're struggling, it means it's not the past. It's all present."

"It's never gonna change, Graham."

"I know. What you feel for Ryan will never die. It's going to stay with you no matter where you go from here, but Ser, it will get easier to handle. You just have to keep fighting."

"What if all my fight is gone? What if it all died with Lucifer?"

"It didn't."

"You don't know that."

"Yes Ser, I do." He says, reaching out to me and pulling me into his arms, my back perfectly aligned with his. "You wouldn't be here at all if you weren't a fighter."

He's got one hand securely wrapped around my stomach but the other one, his fingers are in my hair and it feels like my own personal version of heaven. It's been so long since someone's run their fingers through my hair, especially slow the way he is now. All the tension I felt about coming here and with him at all, is fading away piece by piece with each stoke of his fingers. I can almost believe that everything is all right with the world again.

Except I know it's not. At least it isn't in my world.

"Graham," I whisper, my breath catching in my throat as his hand stops mid stroke on my head, reacting to his name. "Why did you really come back?"

I don't want him to say he came back for me. I want him to say it was school, the damn art program that he claimed was the reason he came here the first time. I'm afraid to hear that it's me because he will have made the trip for nothing. I know how he feels about me, but I will never be able to give him what he deserves. I'm too empty and broken for that now.

"You know why I came back."

"No, I don't. I want you to tell me."

He sighs and my heart aches. He did come back for me, but he doesn't want to admit it because he's aware of how far gone I am. He knows I'm no good for anything or anyone anymore.

"You. I came back for you. When Gabriel told me that you were back, there was no question about where I needed to be. Where I've always needed to be."

I attempt to slide out of his arms, the way I'm cradled now too intense. Sitting like that, having it feel so damn intimate, it's leading him on. It's giving him hope, something I no longer have any of.

"I think we should go back."

"No." When I swivel my head around to look at him, surprised by his reaction, he instantly tries correcting himself. "I mean, not yet. There's still something we've gotta do before we head back."

As I'm about to ask him what he means, he raises the hand that was in my hair toward the sky and I see what he's getting at. He wants to stay until the sun sets. I'm not entirely sure why, but there's no denying that it's sweet. It's also something we've done more than once before. I guess in a way it's our thing.

"You wanna watch the sunset with me? Graham—"

"Serenity, stop reading so much into it." He says, cutting me off. "I want you to be able to talk to the moon again, that's all."

He wants me to talk to the moon? That's what this visit was about? Reliving old times?

"Why would you want to see me do that? Only crazy people talk to the sky, especially when they're not going to get an answer."

"I guess I want crazy."

In the span of less than twenty-four hours, he's managed to make me do things I never thought I'd be able to do again. My cheeks are warm now, and I'm pretty sure if the sun wasn't already going down, he'd be able to catch the color change in them too. I'm blushing.

"What am I gonna do with you, Graham Cracker?" I laugh, forced as always but hoping he won't notice. Anything to deflect away from the blush that's still threatening to overheat me.

"Do you really want me to answer that?"

"I guess not."

"You wanna know what you're gonna do with me? Anything you want. Whatever you feel comfortable with. We can just sit here like this all night," he stops, realizing the distance I put between us and pulling me slowly back to his arms. "Or, we go over there to the swings and go so high we end up getting sick. Hell, I'll even get my huge legs to go down that slide over there. Whatever you want."

"Why are you doing this? Why are you trying so hard?"

"I'm not trying at all. If you wanna see how I act when I actually try, I suppose I can show you, but princess, this is just me being me. This isn't about you."

"Sea of bullshit, Graham."

He leans into me and I can feel his breath hot against my ear. "I know you can swim, Serenity, so if it's bullshit, swim your way out."

That's it. I can't take this anymore. Grabbing the hand that's still resting comfortably around my chest, I lift and drop it, skirting across the grass until we're not connected in any way, getting to my feet and rubbing my hands over my knees the second we're apart.

"What did I say?" he asks, his voice deflated. Hearing him this way just proves my point. I'm hurting him without even trying.

"Nothing. It's nothing. Please take me home now."

Screw the moon, the stars and him wanting to hear me talk to them. I can't be that girl anymore, no matter how right it felt in the moment sitting there. I'm the worst kind of human being. I don't deserve to feel comfortable. This is all wrong. Ryan deserves better. So does Graham.

"If you really wanna go that badly, I'll take you back." He says as he gets to his feet and pushes off the tree, making his way slowly, every step deliberate until he's standing at my side again. "But at some point, you're gonna have to let me in."

"You don't want in, Graham."

"You're wrong. I wouldn't ask if I didn't want to be. You think I don't get what you're doing, but trust me, I get it. You're scared and you have every right to be, but just because you push, kick and scream, doesn't mean things are gonna change. I'm not going anywhere."

The way my heart leaps, grasping onto his words so easily upsets me. I don't want to be happy about him standing his ground and not leaving. He says he understands but he doesn't, not really. He doesn't get that every second he spends with me is one less he's going to have to enjoy his life. He's wasting his time and he doesn't even see it.

"How long have you known me?" he whispers as he leans down.

"Five years."

"Do you trust me?"

"With my life."

"If that's true, then stop running, Ser. Lean on me. Tell me what you're holding on to so tightly that it's twisting you in knots."

Can I do it? Can I really tell him what I'm so scared of? Will doing it make him finally understand and back off the way he needs to?

There's only one way I'm ever going to know. I need to tell him the truth, the way we always have. He deserves to know it all.

"I'm scared that if I let you in, if you stay; what happened to Ryan is going to happen to you and Graham, I can't let that happen again. I can't lose any more of my heart. There's not much left as it is. So just do yourself a favor. Take me home and come back here to your mom. It's where you belong."

I've always been able to sense things with Graham. It wasn't always that way, but the closer we got hanging out during high school, I picked up on his facial expressions and body language easily. He became an open book even though I couldn't reach into his mind. Right now, he's standing completely still beside me, his face is flush, probably because of the quick movement getting up, but otherwise he's a blank slate. I have no idea how he's reacting to what I just said and I'm almost afraid to ask.

His hand, which had been completely rested at his side when he walked over to me, moves and he slides it around mine, connecting our fingers so we're locked together. Again the small touch raises the heat in my body and head at least another hundred degrees.

Damn soul-mate bond. This consistent reaction to him is off putting. I don't know what to do and it's slowly going to end up driving me crazy. Another reason he's better coming back here after he drops me off and staying away.

"What happened to Ryan was not your fault. He was given a choice and he made it. I would have done the same thing if it meant you got to continue living your life. I know what you're afraid of, but I'm only gonna tell you this one more time. There is no place safer for me to be than right where I am now."

"Graham..."

"No Ser. Just listen okay?" he asks and when I nod he sighs. "Two years I spent wondering what happened to you. If you were finally happy now that you were free. Gabriel showing up when he did, giving me a chance to right everything that I turned wrong before you left, was a gift. I had a chance to come back and just be around you again. If you think for a second that I'm gonna let you drive me off because you think you're doing the right thing, you've got another thing coming. I'll take you home alright, but I'm not going anywhere."

"I don't get a say in this, do I?"

"No. Sorry, you don't. If you want to leave right now, I'll take you, but here's what's gonna happen when we get back on campus. We're just going to exist. No noise, talking; unless you want to, nothing. We're just going to do something we've never done. We're just going to be."

I attempt to respond, but his free hand lifts and lays across my lips, preventing me from whatever it is that I'm about to say.

"No more words Ser. Let's just go be."

Chapter Ten

When Souls Collide

Graham

I'm gonna admit it. I have no idea what the hell I'm doing right now. I've never dealt with someone like Serenity before. Every step I take, the words I say, I never know what kind of reaction I'm going to get. All I know is that when she pulls away, it feels like she's yanking a part of me away with her.

We drove the rest of the way back to the dorm in complete silence, but for me at least, it wasn't an uncomfortable one. It felt just as right as everything else has since I showed up in her Psych class this morning. If it's possible it might have felt more right than the rest of it because we were doing what I said I wanted before we left.

Once we were back in her room and she saw for sure that I wasn't going anywhere, having taken up a good half of her bed when I threw myself on it and stretched out, she resigned herself to spending the rest of the night with me. I meant what I said and I wanted her to see how real it was. It might have been smart for me to leave, but I didn't want to. She's been alone long enough.

I don't even care how it makes me look or how much it might annoy her. It's for her own good; our own good. We both need this even though we're both too stubborn to admit it.

I've never come right out and said that I need her. That I need the closeness that being around her provides, at least I haven't since that day where I confessed all before the showdown with Lucifer. I'm stubborn that way, even when it ends up costing me. She'd been away from me for two years because I was too scared and too stubborn to admit that I wanted and needed her just as much as she did me.

That's what she's doing now even though she's putting up with our imposed silence. She's sticking to her guns and stubbornly believing that she needs to go through all of this alone. That having me here will do nothing even though with the changes I've already seen happening in her, it's having the opposite effect.

We need each other. We're always going to need each other and no matter how long it takes, I'm determined to make her see it as clearly as I do now. I'm tired of being stubborn and believing that I can do this life alone or that I can do it without her. I know better now.

"I know you said you wanted us to just be tonight, but if I wanted to talk, would you be upset?"

Timid Serenity. The girl that doubts her every move, including her own words. I haven't seen this girl in so long and having her appear now is just plain wrong. She's so much more than some timid human and I want her to accept that and stop doing this.

"No. I could never be upset with you."

"That might be the first time you've ever told me a lie, Graham."

"What happened that day at the coffee shop notwithstanding," I say, knowing exactly what she's getting at. "There isn't anything you could do that would upset me. If you wanna talk, we can talk."

"Even if you don't like what I've got to say?"

"Yep, even then. What's on your mind?"

"I've been hearing his voice in my head. I don't sleep because when I do, I see us together. He's all I think about, even when I'm sitting here with you. I feel like what we're doing, even though it's not anything bad, is betraying him. I can't do that."

I'm not a big believer in love at first sight. I don't even believe in connections and bonds even though I'm living through a pretty big one right now. I think it's all just attraction. It's human reaction, pure and simple. Love is something that builds from friendship, from time spent, secrets shared, lives lived, not from one look across the room at someone.

It's part of the reason for the fight we had the day she tried telling me about Ryan. I couldn't see how three or four days with a person could be love, or at the very least, a life together. It still makes no sense to me, but seeing her now, the way her whole body seems to sag with the weight of what she's admitting; her eyes vacant again, the loss apparent head to toe, I can't sit here and say that what she's experiencing isn't love.

When she left me, I looked like this. When she walked away two years ago and I refused to reach out and stop her by telling her the truth, I lived this exact same reaction and I know deep inside that what I feel for her is love. I don't have anything to compare it to, but feeling dead inside when the person you care about isn't with you, it can't be anything other than love.

It means that what she and Ryan had is as real as what I feel for her and because of that, I have to look at things differently now. Just because I haven't felt this with anyone else since my time with her doesn't mean that she hasn't.

"I think all of that is natural. I mean, I don't know for sure because I've never been through it, but being unable to let go, being bound to them, when you love someone seems like a normal thing."

"So you think it's okay that I'm experiencing all of this?"

"No, it's not okay. Ser, I don't want you feeling any kind of loss or pain at all, but in order to heal, you've gotta feel something. Numb can only get you so far. It's not pretty but maybe this is your way of coping with what you went through."

"It happened weeks ago. Shouldn't I be over it by now?"

"I can't answer that. Everyone experiences grief differently. I can say that if this was me and I lost you or my mom, I don't think I'd be over it yet. I'm not sure I would ever be over it."

We've been having this heavy conversation and she's on one side of the bed and I've just been lounging on the other, neither one of us looking at the other, just speaking across the bed, but with what I just said, the way of being changes and now I can feel her eyes on me. It's only when I look up and meet them that I see what's there staring me in the face.

They're no longer empty. There's a sheen in them that hasn't been there since I came back. It's one I haven't seen since the last time I stood in this room with her, admitting things two years in the making. She's experiencing my words, feeling things from them and they're softening her, changing her even. Where she was cold before, I can sense warmth again.

She's healing and I don't even think she's aware of it.

"I don't want to lose you, Graham. I don't want to ever be so lost that you can't find me. You should never have to go through this."

"Princess, you're never gonna lose me. I promised you that years ago and I'm doing it now. Our friendship, the way we are with each other, it's never ending."

"Our past lives..." she starts and I raise my hand to stop her.

"I know. We never end up together. We're always pulled apart. I was scared about that when you first told me everything. I didn't want this lifetime to be like the others. I didn't want to face losing you. I still don't want to face that. It's different now though, at least for me. I'm choosing not to look at it like that anymore. Someone told me it was impossible remember?"

Her cheeks flush and my heart hammers out of my chest. I'm starting to feel like Superman with the way I'm getting her to react to me. When I first showed up and saw the vacancy in her eyes, I doubted I would be the right one to break through. I'm not worried about that now. She's still not all the way there, but there's no mistaking that despite her every effort to appear otherwise, she's unable to stop whatever's happening inside of her.

Maybe this soul-mate bond isn't a total waste after all.

"Maybe I was wrong."

"You? Wrong? Since when?"

"Ha-ha. It is possible you know."

"You're not wrong about this." I say, enjoying the momentary break in the seriousness of the conversation. "We're never going to lose each other."

"You promise?"

"Cross my heart and hope to die, princess. I will pinky swear, make a blood promise, whatever it takes."

"Gross. Blood promise?"

"Well I could always get you to spit in your hand, do the same and we could shake on it that way if you want?"

She shakes her head but she's laughing now and again my heart swells. Five years goes by and her laughter, the smile, even that cute little flush she gets in her cheeks still has the ability to turn me inside out. The love I have for this girl is fucking ridiculous.

"Can I tell you something?"

Again her eyes look up and lock on mine as she nods.

"Please don't take this the wrong way, because I know how it's gonna sound, but it's the truth."

"Are you gonna make me wade through bullshit again?"

"Probably." I laugh. "I know what you said that day is the truth because every second I've ever spent with you, before and after we learned the truth, is about as close to Heaven as a person can get when they're living down here."

"What does that mean?"

"It means that we're never gonna lose each other and it's got nothing to do with us being two parts of the same soul. Serenity, it's because you're my Heaven."

Admitting this, I didn't know what to expect. It's heavy and right now, probably not the best thing in the world to say, considering the truth she admitted to me not five minutes ago about the other guy in her life, but I can't hold back. I did that long enough. It's time she knew it all, even if she's not ready.

It's exactly what I thought in the car earlier. I can't do this without my feelings playing a part in it. It's impossible not to feel when I'm with her.

After a few seconds pass without her reacting, I start to think I've pushed her too far, made her shut down again. It's the last thing I want, but before I can clear my throat, turn toward her, touch her in some way to get her to say or do something, she takes me off guard.

Moving from her spot, she straddles her legs over mine and she grips my face with her hands. Catching a glimpse of her before she leans in, I come face to face with another look I haven't seen in her for weeks. Certainty. Determination. I want to react to the look, say something and call attention to it because it's so fucking beautiful, but her lips press themselves to mine before I get the chance.

We're right back in front our houses again, seventeen years old, her buzzed from the beer she drank and me wanting to get her home so she didn't do anything she'd regret in the morning. Her body is pressing to mine differently so I know my vision of the past is melding with the one now, but it feels exactly the same.

Sliding my hand around her head, gripping her hair, I meet her body with my own, craving even more contact between us. Her lips part and a small breathless moan escapes as I crash mine back into hers and all self-control I had falls down around me.

She nips my bottom lip with her teeth before catching it and sucking, a growl escaping from my throat. How long have I waited for her to do this again, to experience the dizziness, the natural buzz that comes whenever we touch so intense I'm drowning in it.

Too damn long.

I need more.

Wrapping my arms around her, I pick her up, my tongue running across her now parted lips pushing for acceptance and bring her back down onto the bed, now positioned above her. Opening my eyes just a little as the kiss deepens, our tongues meeting in a fury, tangled up in each other, fighting for control, I see her own staring back at me, a mixture of pain and pleasure buried in them and it's all I need to see.

Pulling back, allowing the both of us the chance to catch our breath, she slides herself up higher onto the bed, completely silent other than the sound of the creak the bed makes as her body moves with it, her expression unreadable.

"I'm sorry, I don't know what got into me." I say, trying to come up with an explanation for what just happened, what I saw in her eyes before I pulled away, anything that will make this easier for her.

"I do." she says, her fingers now rubbing over the soft lips I just lost myself in, her voice barely audible through her attempt to steady her now erratic breathing.

"You do?"

"Yeah, Graham I do."

"You feel like sharing because that, I didn't want that to happen." I somehow manage to choke out and the minute I do, I feel like shit. It's not what I want to say at all. "I mean, I did, but not that way. I didn't come back for that."

"I know you didn't."

"Then what was that? What are we doing, Ser? What does that kiss mean?"

"It means I'm lost Graham. It means I have no idea what I'm doing anymore, but I'm so damn tired of overthinking things. It means I want to find my way back. I want to be okay again, but I don't think I can do it alone. It's—"

"It's what?"

"It's you."

She's losing me. I'm not sure what she means. Her admitting so freely that she can't do this alone; that she can see what's happening and wanting to change it, I can jump the gun and assume, answer it the way my heart wants me too, but I'm not sure I want to do that and end up being wrong. I need her to tell me what all of this means. I can't move forward until she does.

"Ser, what does that mean? What are you trying to say? I don't wanna read into this, but fuck, that kiss, what I felt, it's kind of hard not to."

"For weeks, all I wanted was to forget. To wake up and find out that all of this was a dream. That I never moved here for school. To get up and see that I was still back home, with you, where everything felt okay. Graham, I don't wanna be alone anymore. I want you to stay, even if I'm scared of what that means."

I can't believe it. This can't be possible. My heart, it's healing and breaking at the exact same time. It's breaking because I know how hard this is for her to admit. How clouded she's been lately, but afraid to break away from it because it's the only tangible thing she has left of Ryan and what they experienced together, yet at the same time healing because she's admitting what I've waited five years to hear.

She needs me, but more than that, she wants me.

Now I just need to make sure that she knows she has me. Always. Our lives, they're meant to be tangled together and there's no way in hell I'm going to pull them apart.

"You're never going to be alone again, Ser. I'm staying for as long as you want me to."

For a split second, I think she's going to cry but just as I reach out in an attempt to catch them before they start, they're gone and her eyes are clear and bright. The way they were before Heaven and Hell had to stake a claim on her life.

"Do you think you can handle forever?"

"Forever and then some."

Lucifer

This is working out even better than I imagined. I have learned so many things just watching these two when they made their way back to campus that I have no doubt the path that I have put myself on is the right one. It is only a matter of time now before I can bring myself completely out of hiding and bring about the end that should have happened months ago.

Graham Hudson is more than just a vessel Gabriel used in an effort to get closer to Serenity. He is so much more and given the information that I had previously gone by, it changes everything, but not in a drastic way. It just means that instead of only going after Serenity, I could also go for the other half of her soul in the process.

It was my belief that she had no soul mate. Given her allegiance to the light, being born of Heaven and all the power she holds inside her, it seemed only fair that she not be on the receiving end of a bond of that nature. I could not have been more wrong. She has a soul-mate and one with surprising strength and light inside of him.

Now not only would I bring Heaven to its knees by attacking their treasured ball of light, but I would also do the same to Serenity by destroying the very reason her heart continues to beat.

There is no bond greater on the human plain than that of the soul-mate. It is an honor that not all human beings get to experience, but one that is so powerful once it has been realized that it is almost impossible to tear apart. They are the same soul, just split apart in an effort to gain knowledge, learning in different ways for my father. When their time was done, their goals completed, they would once again be joined together, never to be torn apart again.

As the two of them embrace now, completely unaware that they are being watched, it makes the end result that much clearer. I am doing the right thing with the plan I have put into motion. It is only a matter of time before their precious little bubble bursts and Serenity's past and future collide.

All that is left now is to bide my time, waiting patiently for the attachment between these two to grow even deeper than it already appears to be and the timing will be perfect. This time, I will bring about true hell on earth and there is not a being or person above or below that will stop me.

Chapter Eleven

Revelations

Gabriel

Things have changed.

When I arrived here this morning to find Serenity with Graham, the both of them sleeping in her bed; arms wrapped around one another, I was not sure how I felt about it and it had nothing to do with the short burst of jealousy I experienced at first sight.

It has to do with what Graham told me before he made his way back to her. He assured me that this would not happen because of the way he feels toward her and that he would go through with this, make it happen in a more basic way. The way they find themselves now, it stands to reason that he had not kept his word.

The way the bond works between Serenity and myself, we are to be the complete opposite of one another. Where I am guided by my emotions, able to feel far more than any of my brothers or even other humans that inhabit the earth, she would experience far less. She would be more action oriented, thinking with her head more than her heart.

I am having such a hard time with the way I saw them this morning because it appears as though it works the same way with them. Graham may not have wanted to go into this based on his emotions or even the bond between them, but in the end, it had to be that way in order for him to break through. He is offering her what I cannot.

He is not supposed to be doing things this way. They are already two halves of the same whole, which means he is most like her, more action oriented and less reliant on the emotional end of things. Appearing to be more like me just makes me want to appear before them both and break them apart.

"Jealousy does not become you brother."

"Surely you can sympathize with my plight."

"I can. Graham being more like you than her is not the way that it should be, but you can see how that seems to work well with the way things have been thus far."

"What is that supposed to mean?"

"From the moment this undertaking began, nothing has gone according to plan. You allowed yourself to be manipulated by Lucifer; Serenity chose a path that she was never meant to take and we lost one of our own in the fight. Though with that last one, we were unaware of it at the time. It seems only fitting that this work the same way."

"Well, it matters little. Once we appear before them and explain all that we know, both of Lucifer and Ryan, things will surely go back to the way they have been."

"Why do I get the feeling that you are looking forward to that?"

"I have no idea. I do not gain pleasure from watching anyone suffer, least of all Serenity and Graham. You know what they both have come to mean to me."

"I am aware of what they mean to you, but if Serenity reacts the way that we expect her to, then doesn't that mean she will pull away from Graham and back into herself again? Would that not also mean you would be able to reach out to her and bring her around to your way of being?"

"You are overthinking things Michael. I have never once looked at it that way."

"Gabriel, you forget that I know you far better than you do yourself. Lying will get you nowhere. It might have been able to work on those two sleeping humans down there, but it never works on me."

"I am not lying."

"Yes, you are and you have just proven it. You're lying to yourself because you have indeed thought about this. It's why when I mentioned what would happen the minute they learn the truth, there was the faintest trail of a smile on your face."

"Is there even a point to telling you that you're wrong?"

"No, because I'm not wrong."

"Fine. I don't like her this close with Graham. It is merely because of the bond we share. The very bond that I need to put out of my mind so that moving forward we are able to keep a clear head."

"Are you going to be able to do that?"

"To quote the most annoying archangel I know; *'I will do whatever is needed'*."

"Cute, Gabriel. That's pretty good advice. You should definitely take it."

"As beautiful as this scene is, I do believe it is time that we got on with the reason we're here. We do not have much time before Father realizes that we have blocked him out and gone against his direct orders, so the sooner we inform them, the better for all of us."

"We're paying for this no matter what. Let's just give them a few more minutes. They're so peaceful right now. Other than my time with Faith, it's probably the most peaceful scene I have ever come across."

"You enjoy torturing me don't you?"

"Immensely." He laughs before pointing at the two sleeping forms in front of us, who are now beginning to awaken from their slumber. "It appears as though I'm going to have to find another way to accomplish it though. It's time."

"Thank God."

"Now, now Gabriel. Father has nothing to do with this and I am pretty sure that when he does learn of it, the last thing you are going to want to do is thank him."

I have heard more than enough of this. Michael had been the one to come down and inform me that we needed to tell them the truth. Wasting time making jokes about everything I am going through watching Graham and Serenity together is not getting us anywhere.

"Oh Gabriel, cheer up. We're about to tell your beloved that again we've managed to turn her entire life upside down. Graham will be a thing of the past soon enough."

As we move forward, Michael's words haunt me. I know they are wrong and that the last thing I want is Serenity to feel any more darkness and pain. I cannot escape it though. The rush of excitement I experience at his final words. Graham and Serenity being torn apart, it brings me joy and there is nothing I can do to tame it.

I am no longer able to focus on the hurt she is about to experience. Only the happiness that I will achieve being the one to make it happen.

Serenity

"Think about what you're saying. What it really means. I'm going to have to marry you in one of the darkest ceremonies known to all humankind and once we do that, drain you of your power. Of the light inside you. The goodness. You'll be lost to me. We will never be able to go back."

"So we don't go back. I know what I'm saying Ryan and I know how much you wish I wasn't saying it, but if all we have is a few hours before he comes and takes me anyway, we might as well accept it and move forward. I want to do this. Please let me do this."

"I don't think I can. Serenity, before I allowed the darkness to become such a big part of my life, I spent every second praying to meet the one person in the world that would save me from feeling so alone. I've finally done that. I've found you. Please don't make me give you up."

"Don't you see? If we go through with this, then you won't be giving me up. Yes, I will lose myself, at least the human parts of me, but no one can take me away entirely. I want to do this. Let me do this. Let me be with you in the only way possible."

~*~*~

"In his own way, Gabriel loves you. He's wanted nothing more in the last twenty years then to protect you from this very thing. Then there's me. I think I've already told you how I feel, but if you want to hear more, I've got no problem telling you. I was awake in Emma's bed last night after you passed out in my arms. I got to experience the way it felt having you pressed up against me. The way your heartbeat seemed to slow to a crawl while you slept, probably the most peaceful you have in years. If I didn't love you before that moment, I damn sure did then."

~*~*~

Well that's a first.

Not only are my feelings conflicted when I'm awake but now it seems like it's carrying over to when I'm sleeping too. Waking up, the reality crashing into me as it usually does that everything I just experienced was a replay of the past, only a dream, I felt guilty for being thankful.

In times past I've had nightmares like this, remembering moments with Ryan as if they're happening for the very first time and woken up covered in sweat, screaming or crying out for the boy that's no longer here to answer my call. This time though, it shifted from Ryan to Graham so effortlessly that I'm thankful for it.

I turn over in the bed and instead of coming face to face with the wall the way I'm expecting, Graham's still form is there to greet me, reminding me again of the night before, what we talked about and even more than that, what we shared together. Waking up and seeing him, his confession of love, what he felt the last time we'd been in a bed together, it comforts me in a way I never thought possible with the way the last few weeks have been. My heart is completely at rest, relaxed, no longer pounding to the beat of its own drum and it's all because of him.

I'm not deluded enough to think that things will be better than they were. Dreaming about Ryan proves that I'm not at that point yet, but the reprieve I get waking up the way a normal person does, not having to worry about who might hear my cries or experience the madness going on in my head, it's a small blessing.

That's where the guilt comes in. In waking up this way, I feel like I'm breaking free of the memories I have with Ryan, in some way forgetting him and I don't want to do that. He might be gone and I probably do need to move on from it, time healing all wounds and all, but forgetting the way it felt being around him, I don't wanna lose that. I don't ever wanna lose him.

Despite the guilt, I still reach out to Graham, wrapping my arm around his chest and curving my body into his. With him asleep, I don't have to worry about his reaction and right now I need that. I just want to enjoy what it feels like being this close to someone again. Being this close to him.

How many times have we done this before? Falling asleep while hanging out together, waking up in the morning, blushing, trying to hide the way we feel from each other and going on like nothing happened? There's been so many I've lost count. It's the most natural thing in the world for us. What's not natural is how tightly I'm wrapped up in him. Any time we've woken up together this way, it's been unintentional.

This time it's intentional and despite how shitty I feel for even thinking it, I want more. Even being this close to him isn't close enough.

His body shifts under my arm and I know he's waking up. Attempting to slide my arm out before he realizes what I've done, I feel a tightness around my wrist and realize instantly I've been caught.

"Keep it there." He says sleepily, going even further and pulling it tighter around his frame, which both excites and frightens me. Being this way with Graham, it's so damn right and wrong.

"We've got class in an hour."

Way to go Serenity. Could you be any more awkward right now? The last thing you should be mentioning right now is class. Who cares about class?

"Hmmm, I vote for being no shows."

He releases my hand as his body shifts and he's turned around facing me. Smiling before closing his eyes again he reaches for my hand and places it up against his heart. This is killing me. It's too close. I know what I told him last night, but this, I'm not ready for this yet. I don't know if I ever will.

"Graham..." I sigh, attempting again to pull away. This time he seems to pick up on it because he lets me go easily and again I'm torn up inside because I hate how easily he lets go and that it even has to happen at all.

"I'm sorry. Didn't think."

"You don't have to be sorry, I should be apologizing to you."

He's more aware now, his eyes completely open and staring right back into mine, full of questions, ones I don't know if I can answer.

"No, you don't. You asking me to stay, I know what it means. We've got all the time in the world Serenity."

"It's really that simple for you?"

"Yeah. I've been in love with you since I was sixteen years old. I'm twenty-one now. Five years, Ser Bear. If I can go that long, I think I can go another five, ten, or twenty. Whatever you need."

I want to tell him he won't have to wait that long. That him being here now, what it means, I know it won't take nearly that long, but I can't because then I wouldn't be telling him the truth. I know how I feel about Graham, it's never changed even when Ryan came into my life. It just wasn't as magnified as it was before, but even knowing that, I can't give him hope for something when I don't have any to begin with.

"You'd really wait that long?"

"I'd wait forever."

My gaze falls as I let the gravity of his words sink in. I can't let him wait forever. I can't make him wait at all. It's unfair.

He's one of the most beautiful human beings on the planet, there's gotta be a girl out there for him that isn't riddled under the weight of the destruction she's caused. He would be better off without me.

"That wasn't supposed to make you scowl, ya know. Don't most girls like hearing things like that?"

"I'm not most girls."

"That's true. It's the reason why waiting forever is easy, because you aren't like anyone else in the world."

The room which until now has been shaded in darkness due to the lack of light, explodes in a kaleidoscope of color and it doesn't take me long to figure out why. As much as I hate having to deal with them right now, they couldn't have planned a more perfect time to visit. With what Graham just said, I need the interruption.

Graham turns and brings his body up in the bed, knowing that we've been interrupted, his face showing exactly what he thinks about it too. If I wasn't so weighed down by his words, I might actually share the annoyed sentiment.

I can easily tell its Gabriel, but he's not alone. He's brought another angel with him and it's the very last one I want to see.

Michael. The archangel that told me what happened to Ryan. What I caused by agreeing to Lucifer's plan. The one angel that could remind me of exactly what I lost and all that I've been ignoring getting so caught up in Graham.

"I apologize for the interruption, but Serenity, there is something that we must speak with you about."

There's a light squeeze on my shoulder and as I turn in reaction to it, I see Graham's smiling face looking back at me. Mouthing the words, not wanting the angels to hear me, I ask him to stay and he just nods in response, following it up with another squeeze. Where minutes ago I wanted a break from him, from the things he was saying, feelings he was bringing to the surface, now I can't bear the thought of him walking from the room and leaving me alone with these two.

"Graham stays. You say whatever you have to with him here or you can leave the same way you came."

"Looks like someone got their attitude back." Michael quips and I roll my eyes in response. The differences between him and Gabriel are like night and day. I can get annoyed with Gabriel the same way I can his brother, but not nearly to the degree I am now. Why is he even here to begin with?

"I am here because Gabriel is going against our father and Heaven to appear this way and tell you this. I will not let my brother take the fall alone."

Having no response but still not liking one bit that he's here I roll my eyes again and I hear Graham laugh softly beside me, his grip never once lightening on my shoulder, something I'm enjoying a little too much.

"Just say whatever it is you're going against Heaven to say and get out of here. I told you before, I don't want to be around anyone."

"You certainly seem to have no problem spending time with that particular being."

"Michael, that's enough. You are only making a difficult situation that much worse." Gabriel says and I can feel my resolve softening. I know Gabriel, I know him well despite our awkward history. He wouldn't go against what I asked of him unless it were serious.

"You are right about that Serenity. I am concerned for your well-being but not enough to go against your wishes. I told you I would stand down from visiting you and I meant it."

"Thank you."

"You are most welcome."

"So, someone wanna stop dancing around the reason you're here and bring it up or are we just going to go around in circles?" Graham interjects and I swear there's a second where I see Gabriel's eyes flash dark before they even out and everything appears the way it always does.

What the hell was that? Since when do archangel's eyes go dark?

"Since my brother has learned the human act of jealousy. Not that it matters to you, but the both of you, the way you are, it causes him distress."

"Enough Michael!" Gabriel yells, his voice booming through the room, making me feel even more closed in then I did when they arrived.

"Gabe, you said you had something you needed to tell me. How about we focus on that and ignore everything else?" I ask, my voice low and even. I can feel the tension from here and if there's any truth to what Michael said, focusing attention on it is only going to make it worse.

"Yes. We should do that." He agrees before casting one final look toward Michael and turning back to face me. "As you are aware, when you sent me away, I went home. It was during my time there that I learned of some things. Things that have to do with you and also with Ryan. They will not be easy to hear and even though Father does not wish for me to tell you, I feel that keeping it would only make things worse."

"What about Ryan?" Graham speaks up, bringing my attention away from Gabriel and again back on him. Hearing him say Ryan's name, it's weird. With the way they both feel about me, its strange hearing any of them talk about each other. Like it shouldn't be happening.

"Brother, if I may interrupt you for a moment." Michael says, moving closer to the bed, causing me to slink backwards toward the headboard and closer to Graham, which he gladly accepts as he opens his arms wide enough for me to fit right in.

"Do what you must, Michael."

"I do believe that before we inform them of what we learned about Ryan; more focus needs to be put on the other thing we learned as it is the far more pressing matter at hand."

"What does he mean by that?"

"Lucifer did not perish in the church. He is indeed alive and planning on coming for you again." Gabriel answers, picking up right where Michael left off. "We do not know more than that at the present time, but there is a strong force of evil and it has us all on guard. Until we can ascertain exactly what is going on, you and Graham both need to proceed with caution."

"Yeah, because you know, we're so good at throwing caution to the wind." Graham says which just makes me laugh.

He's got a point. We've been living our lives on edge for weeks now. It's gotten to a point where I'm looking over my shoulder everywhere I go even though I had no idea about any of this.

"There is no need for sarcasm, Graham. We are merely telling you the way things are. You should heed our warning instead of poking fun at it."

"I'll get right on that Mike."

"Gabriel, why do we bother with this at all? We could have easily watched over them from Heaven and them be none the wiser. I refuse to subject myself to this attitude."

Michael is irritated, which isn't exactly surprising. I spent enough time around him when I was healing in Heaven. He's got that kind of air about him. He seems annoyed by all things human or emotionally based in general. Honestly, he's kind of a dick.

"Watch your language ball of light. You might mean something to our father, but you mean very little to me."

"Michael, I will not say this again. You must not let them get to you."

"So Lucifer isn't dead like we thought we was. We mourned him and he's still out there somewhere plotting how he's going to finish what he started in the church. I'll be more careful. What did you learn about Ryan?"

I know it seems like I don't care about the fallen angel and his plans for me. I almost went to my death in an effort to follow through with his dark plan, yet here I am acting like none of it matters at all. I do care, but I'm still so numb inside from the aftermath that I can't seem to focus on anything but what else they're keeping from me.

"It will not be easy to hear, Serenity. You will not like it and you may even wish I had never brought it to your attention at all."

"Just spit it out, Gabe. He's dead. It doesn't get worse than that. I can handle whatever else you have to say unless you're here to tell me he's not actually dead."

"I am afraid I cannot tell you that. Ryan, he was not as he appeared to be, at least not entirely."

"What does that mean?"

"There was a mistake made in Heaven twenty-two years ago. It is one that not even Father knew about until it was too late to do anything about it. It involved Ryan."

Ryan told me how he came to be. I know that he was born because his mother slept with a demon, one that was pretty high up in Lucifer's army. He exists because she hadn't been able to keep her legs closed when the darkness came calling. What any of this has to do with Heaven, I don't get.

"Ryan was not just a hybrid demon, Serenity. He was pure angel, or at least he should have been. He was not slotted to be sent down here but through one wrong move that is exactly what happened. His pure way of being was implanted into a young infant that was born to Corinne McGregor."

"He was what?" Graham asks as I sit locked in his arms, frozen by what Gabriel's just said. I need to be the one asking these questions, but I don't think I can even find the words.

Ryan, my Ryan wasn't supposed to be what he ended up becoming? He wasn't supposed to be a part of this with Lucifer. The only reason he was even around me at all is because Heaven screwed up. If what Gabriel is saying right now is true than it means we never should have interacted with each other at all. He was meant to stay in Heaven.

"No, he was not meant to remain in Heaven. He had a purpose. Being a pure angel, he is the only being in existence able to defeat Lucifer with the level of power our fallen brother has gotten his hands on in the last century or so. He still would have made his way down here."

"I don't get it..."

"The two of you were never slated to cross paths. It is only because of the mix-up, him being sent down and the prayers that he put forth for years as a young boy that the two of you became connected."

"What does that mean exactly?"

"It means that we heard his prayers. What he believed you to be before he passed, you were never meant to be, but you became the minute we screwed up. You really were the answer to his prayers and he to yours, though in the beginning it was supposed to be the man now sharing your bed that answered yours."

"Then how did it become Ryan?"

"That is something I cannot answer. Only Father knows the truth behind it. All I am aware of is that your heart called for something more. The soul-mate bond was not enough to answer your particular call."

"Him being a pure angel means he still would have gone against Lucifer right? It just would have happened at another time."

"Correct." Michael says and I want to strangle him the second he speaks. For some reason it was much easier hearing all of this from Gabe. Having him speak up now when he's the last person I want to hear from, I've never been so angry in my life.

"Let Gabriel tell me."

"At some point you are going to have to stop blaming me for the loss of the hybrid. You did not cause it any more than we did."

"Except you just admitted that you did." Graham says. "You just told us that Heaven screwed up, which means everything that happened in the church that night never should have happened at all. You did cause this."

He's right. Michael and Gabriel might not have been the ones to make the mistake, but whoever did had put us all on this course and now there was nothing we could do to change it. Ryan had met his end way before he was meant to. It didn't help me feel any less guilty, especially knowing that we were the answer to each other's prayers, but the way I felt before, drowning in it, believing I was completely at fault for everything, it's fading.

"I do not think your opinion matters here, human."

"I've got a name ya know."

"I am well aware of that fact Graham Michael Hudson. It does not change what I believe, so please refrain from speaking at all."

"You're an asshole you know that?"

"I have heard far worse from far better."

"The both of you need to stop speaking to one another right now!" Gabriel speaks up and if I wasn't seeing it with my own eyes I wouldn't believe it. They both back down and the room falls completely silent.

"Graham is right." Gabriel continues. "Heaven did make this error and put the events that happened in Green Haven in motion. Serenity still would have found her way to that church, but it would have been under different circumstances. She never would have known of Ryan because Ryan as he was would not exist."

"So if he's a pure angel," I interrupt, needing answers more than a history lesson. "Does that mean he's still in Purgatory or did he end up back home where he belongs?"

That's when it happens. I see Gabriel's face express pain for the first time since he started coming to me months ago. He doesn't even have to say a word, his eyes, the way his face contorts says it all.

"He ceased to exist, Serenity. I am so very sorry,"

The knife that I've been shoving into my own chest for what feels like forever is finally being driven in one more time. I would never admit it, but there was this small part of me that held out hope that one day I would see Ryan again. If he was in Purgatory, I would find a way to break him out and in the end we would be together again. It might not be the things fairy-tales are made of but it would be uniquely us.

Gabriel saying what he did, seeing it written all over his face, even experiencing it deep in my bones, it's taken that last dash hope I had and brought it crashing down around me, smashing it into a million little pieces. There really is no hope left for a happy ending anymore.

The archangel just killed it and me in the process.

"I did no such thing. Serenity, I know how you must feel with what you've just learned but you cannot give up. If you do that than Lucifer wins."

"Gabriel, what is she thinking?" Graham asks, turning toward me, his face twisted with worry.

"She is merely experiencing exactly what I thought she would. I took the last bit of hope she had from her admitting what Ryan's true end was."

"As with all the other humans, it appears as though your girlfriend here believes Gabriel has killed her."

I'm fully expecting Graham to react to Michael's claims, pulling me to him even more or even going so far as to push me away, but he does neither. Instead his head lifts away from where it was resting against mine and he levels the archangel with a look so angry I'm afraid that at any second he's gonna explode.

"For a guy that spends ninety percent of his time hanging out with his daddy, you sure seem to think you know a whole lot about us. She loved him you asshole. So maybe instead of just making assumptions and treating us all like we're pieces of shit, you might try sympathizing with that for once."

"I suggest you watch your tone with me."

"And if I don't? What are you gonna do? Smite me? Go ahead. I refuse to respect you when you won't do the same."

"Graham..."

He turns his eyes back to me now and I see that the second he does, the anger is gone and he's back to normal even though his body is still tense. His green eyes, they're lighter, softer and it's all for me.

"What princess?"

"I've heard enough. I want to go to class now."

"Are you sure?"

"Yes. Please get me out of here. I can't hear anymore. I've had enough."

"Serenity—"

"No Gabe. I've heard enough. Thank you for telling me all of this because you were right, I did need to know, but I can't take anymore right now. Graham and me, we've got class in like twenty minutes and we're still dressed in our stuff from last night. We need to get ready and go. I can't do this with you anymore. Please take Michael and go."

I'm not even sure where those words came from, but I know they needed to be said. I'm thankful that I know the truth now because it makes everything seem a little more right again. I always knew Ryan was more than just some demon hybrid the way Gabriel the rest of Heaven made him out to be. I saw it right from the start. Knowing I was right, what I saw wasn't an illusion, it makes me feel better, but still hurt. Wounded because he died before he had the chance to learn it too.

The minute both angels take their leave of the room, I turn to Graham and squeeze his hand, my weak wordless attempt at letting him know that I'm alright.

"Let's go to class."

"Ser—are you sure that's really what you want to do right now?"

"You told me something yesterday and even though I'm still not totally behind it, you were right and it's time I start living it, especially now."

"What did I say?"

"You said Ryan wouldn't want me living like this, doing this to myself and you're right, he wouldn't. I still think I'm the cause of this and that's not going to change overnight but knowing what I do now, knowing I was right about him all along...Graham I owe it to him to try and be better. So that's what I'm going to do. Starting now."

"So living for him means Psych class?"

"What better place to start over than there? It's where it all started."

Chapter Twelve

Taking Chances

Graham

She hasn't said a word since we left her room and made our way to class and it's bothering me. What she learned, it can't be easy, but where I expected her to crack, show some kind of reaction toward it, she hasn't and it's not like her.

Serenity has never been the emotional type. All those years she spent hearing voices, being put into a center because her mom didn't understand what she was dealing with, if she had been emotional before, going through that changed her. She kept things inside, she let them fester until they escaped without her consent or control. Being that way, I should have seen this coming, but the way she's been since I came back, more emotional than before, I expected more.

Everyone has a point they reach where they can't take any more and shut down. I'm sure that's what's going on right now. I shouldn't be worried about it, but I am. I mean it can't make her feel great knowing that Ryan wasn't really meant to be a demon and Heaven dropped the ball.

The only thing that shows me she's still with me is what happens when we get to class. As I'm about to take the seat behind her again, she shakes her head and points to the chair across from her. Ryan's seat. It's been vacant since the last time they were in class together before everything came to a head and she hasn't let anyone take it.

Until now.

It might seem insignificant to most people, her giving me this seat, but it means everything. The things she said to me before Gabriel and Michael left, she's putting truth to them now. If she wants to start living again, there's no better way to do that then let up on the hold she has on the seat he used to occupy. The thing is, where she seems okay with me taking it, I'm not sure I feel all that great about it.

I'm pretty sure it's not her intent but in taking his seat, which I eventually do, it feels like I'm stepping into the role of replacement. I don't want to be her second choice. With what we shared this morning, I want to be her only choice. Yet here I am, uncomfortable as hell, overthinking everything and feeling like I'm stepping in until someone better comes along. Until Ryan comes back even though we know that's impossible.

Feeling uncomfortable, it's not just about where I'm sitting and who the seat used to belong to. I'm all torn up inside because that's not the only thing I learned today. Lucifer is still out there somewhere and at any point he could make a play for her and there's not a damn thing I can do to stop him. With the way Gabriel described the power he has, it means that a human like me wouldn't even give him the equivalent of a paper cut.

I've always wanted to keep her safe, be her rock when she needs it and fight whatever and whoever I had to in order to make sure that nothing ever hurt her, but this...I can't do it. I'm not an angel, I'm not a half demon. All I am is a run of the mill guy who just happens to be in love with a ball of heavenly light. If push came to shove she would be the one protecting me and I hate it.

I might not be able to do anything spectacular in terms of keeping her safe from the devil, but there is something I can do better than anyone. In fact, I think right now, I'm the only one that's close enough to be able to make it happen.

She wants to start living again, stepping out of the box she's had herself locked up tightly in for weeks. I can give that to her. This is where my focus needs to be. Not on taking Ryan's place or my lack of supernatural power. Definitely not in this class right now learning about something I don't even care about.

"Hey." I whisper and when her head lifts from the book she's reading, a tiny smile creeping across her face, I know I'm doing the right thing. "You think you can take notes for me?"

"Um, why do you want me to do that?"

"There's something I need to do. I spaced on it earlier, but if I don't do it now, I don't know when I'm gonna get the chance again."

"That's all you're gonna tell me?"

"Not much more to say. So, can you do it?"

"Yeah Graham, I can do it but you owe me."

"I'll tell you everything when we meet up after class. Promise." I slide myself out of the seat and bend over her head, pressing my lips to the top of her hair, breathing in her strawberry scent before kissing softly. "You're the best."

There's no guarantee this idea of mine is going to work, but there's no going back now. I only hope that when I come find her after class and explain, it works out the way I want it to.

If she's going to start living again then the best way to do that is by doing something she's never done. I'm going to help her start living again by giving her something back that I'm sure she didn't even know she was missing.

Serenity

Something's going on with Graham.

I saw the way he reacted when I told him to take Ryan's seat but I think he's reading too much into it. I've been holding on to that seat and the memories attached to it for so long now that in order to get past everything I've been through, what I learned today, I need to release the hold I've got on it.

Giving up the seat doesn't mean that I forget him or even the words exchanged between us when he sat there. It just means that I'm willing to see now how unhealthy my attachment to it has been and the time has come for me to do something about it. If I'm serious about changing, living my life again, it all starts here.

Waking up with Graham this morning, falling asleep with him the night before, opening myself up after a self-imposed silence, it seems almost too good to be true, but I meant what I said to him. I want him to stay. I'm better when he's with me and I don't care how that makes me look. Maybe Graham is a crutch for me, something I can use to forget what I shared with Ryan, but that's not how I look at him. He was the first guy to break through my walls, the first person besides Emma that I allowed myself to have feelings for. If anything Ryan was the crutch to get over Graham.

I hate myself for thinking that way because it's not at all true, but based on the way my life has gone so far, it's not like I can deny it.

I'm pretty sure him leaving class has to do with me giving him Ryan's seat. I don't think he liked it much. It's a guy thing. Even with Ryan gone, I get the feeling that Graham might feel like he's in competition with him even though that's the furthest thing from the truth. They're nothing alike and they mean different things to me. Graham isn't just the first boy I loved, he's my best friend. What I share with him is different yet just as important as what I shared with Ryan during our short time together, maybe even more.

There's something about any time I spend with him that is just so inherently right. Other than the one time outside English Lit where we came across each other after the two year absence, I have never been afraid to be with him. It's always been comfortable and we just flow easily into this routine with each other that no one that comes after him can ever touch.

As great as everything felt with Ryan, it wasn't that way with him. Even finding out how much we had in common, how attached I became to him in such a short period of time, it was never easy. We had Lucifer and the angels in our way the entire time.

I want things to be easy again. Lucifer may not have died and he could very well be watching me right now, but I can't focus all my attention on it. If I do that, then what I told Graham this morning will be a lie. I wouldn't be living again, or if I was it would be living in fear and not for the right reasons. I want the ease that comes with waking up every morning, taking in a breath of the air around me and feeling excited to start the day.

Going from classes to the coffee shop, hell, even to the movies or dinner and not thinking about what part I'm gonna play in the world not ending. For the first time since I learned what I really am, I want to put it out of my mind altogether and experience what it feels like to be uniquely human.

Screw it. If he doesn't wanna be here then neither do I. I'm gonna find out what that weird expression on his face was when he asked if I could take notes for him. I'm going to find out why he kissed my hair the way he did before he left. I'm not going to able to rest until I do.

Scooping up my books, I slide myself out of the seat and start taking the steps quickly until I'm at the front of the room and a few seconds away from the door and relative freedom. When Gabriel dropped me back here, I was determined to throw myself back into my classes, never missing one unless it was life or death, determined to just go through the motions until the pain stopped.

The pain might still be resting there on the periphery in my mind, waiting for the chance to push itself to the forefront again, but I'm ready for it now. I'll deal with it when it comes because now I've got a mission and nothing is going to take me away from it.

The time for routines is over. It's time to live and I know just where to start.

Graham

It doesn't take long once I get out of the class and make my way across campus to Serenity's dorm for me to be let in. I noticed it the first time I showed up here, the lack of security they had considering it was a girl's dorm, but had been more caught up in reconnecting with Serenity again and not about what it all meant in the long term.

Now though, knowing what kind of evil is truly lurking out there, getting into this dorm so easily is leaving me unsettled. It's definitely something I'm gonna have to talk to Serenity about once I've done what I came here to do.

There's only one person on the entire campus that I know and considering that I haven't spent a whole lot of time here since Gabriel came calling months ago, she's the only person I can bring this too. Leaving Serenity in class in order to come back and attempt to reach out to her roommate isn't exactly making me feel the best, but if Emma could do what I needed than it would all work out in the end.

Knocking on the door and taking a few steps back in preparation of the door opening, I'm actually shocked by how quickly it happens. With everything Serenity told me about Emma, the girl doesn't make a point of getting out of bed before noon most days, and it's definitely a lot earlier than noon.

"Yeah, what do you want?" she asks, rubbing at her eyes, blinking a bunch before finally settling and taking me in. "Shit, Graham?"

"Was wondering if you were gonna realize it."

"What are you doing here? Aren't you supposed to be in class or something?"

"Aren't you?"

"Good point. If you're looking for Serenity, I think she already left for Psych. I came in after her so I'm not sure but since she's been doing the same shit for weeks, I figure that's where she is now."

"I know where she is. I'm here to talk to you."

"Me?"

"Yes, Emma. As hard as it is to believe, there are some things that I can't go to Serenity about which leaves me here waking you up."

"You not being here about something related to our best friend is laughable Graham, but fine, come in and tell me what you need my help with."

Making my way into the room, I head for Serenity's bed. It's not the liveliest part of the room, but it is the side that will give me the connection with her that I seem to crave so badly.

It's been this way since I woke up beside her this morning. Feeling her arm wrapped around me, how at first I thought I was dreaming until she attempted to move it away. That small bit of contact sparked something in me that I haven't felt since she left two years ago. I need to be around her, even if right now all I can do is be around her stuff.

"How much do you know about Stephenville?"

"Ugh, not a history lesson. If you wanna know about the town, go to the library Hudson."

"I mean, places to go; things to do and I don't mean the movie and dinner thing."

"Is this your way of asking me to help you plan something for Ser?"

"Yeah. I want to do something with her that we haven't done before, but my lack of knowledge about this place is screwing with me. I can easily find restaurants or theatres and just do what everyone else does, but I want to do something that has meaning."

"Are you sure she's going to wanna do something with you? Look, I'm not trying to be a bitch, but you haven't been here the last few weeks. You haven't seen the Serenity that I have. Something inside her, it broke after Ryan did what he did to her. She's not the same anymore."

"What do you mean what Ryan did to her?"

"Bastard kissed and ditched her. She won't tell me anything more than that, but trust me, that's all I need to know. He was a first class jerk and now he seems to have up and vanished on top of it. I mean how sleazy can you get?"

Well, there's no doubt about where Emma's loyalties lie or her hatred for Ryan, though she seems to have no knowledge about what really happened between the two of them. I'm definitely gonna watch my step around her. For whatever reason I was allowed to know all the supernatural stuff and with Emma not knowing, anything I say could come back to bite me and Serenity.

"Yeah, um...I can't really say much about that. I did the same thing."

"Exactly my point. If what Ryan did screwed with her this badly, how do you think you'll get through?"

"Because despite what I did back then, I love her. I want the best for her and she knows that. We're best friends the same way the two of you are. I know the way she's been, I've seen it since I got back a couple days ago. I want to help her, but in order for me to do that, I need your help first."

"Alright, so you wanna do something different right? That means movies, dinner and parties are all off the table. It doesn't exactly leave much to do."

"There's gotta be something."

"Well the community center runs dance classes every afternoon. One of the girls I party with tried to talk her boyfriend into going to one with her. It didn't work out but I remember her telling me about it. So there's that. Um, there's the zoo, the marina, there's this pond not far from campus. You could take her to church."

Yeah, taking Serenity anywhere near a church wasn't going to happen. I think we've both had our fill of churches for a lifetime, but Emma has given me a few ideas I can work with. Two in particular.

"There's a drive-in not too far from here. I've been there a few times, usually when they're showing eighties flicks. It's pretty secluded and romantic."

"I'm pretty sure secluded and romantic aren't what Serenity needs right now. I just want to take her somewhere quiet, a place where we can hang out together without the pressure of the past if you get what I mean."

"Yeah I get it. You wanna break her of the McGregor effect. It's cool. He never went to any of those places with her. I think they only ever hung out on campus."

"Well, I've got everything I need. I think I can take the rest from here. Sorry for waking you up, but I didn't know where else to go."

"I think you know by now how I feel about Serenity, Graham. If you're here to help her, to bring her back to us then I really don't care about being woken up. Can you do me a favor though?"

"What's that?"

"This time, do things differently. You broke her heart two years ago and it took a really long time for it to heal. Ryan did that for her even if he was a total douchebag in the end. The last thing I want to see is for it to happen all over again. If you're here because you want to be with her, then make sure it sticks this time or I have no problem finding you and kicking your ass."

As much as I hate hearing the truth about what happened between us, she's right. I need to do things differently. I wouldn't repeat the way things were before. Serenity wasn't the only one looking for a new beginning.

I am too.

Serenity

What the hell is going on here?

I managed to catch sight of him as he made his way across campus and keeping myself at a safe distance, I saw him head up the steps to my dorm. If that wasn't bad enough, not only did he go into the dorm but he went straight for my room.

After standing outside the door for a while, I made my way back downstairs and outside, willing to wait him out and catch him when he walked back out but with the more time that passes, I'm beginning to wonder if he's ever going to come out of the room at all.

What could he possibly want in my room? With the way Emma has been lately, going to parties, staying out all night and then coming back in the early hours of the morning and passing out until the late afternoon, I've got no doubt that she's home now but what her and Graham have to say to each other, I have no idea.

I hate that this makes me feel jealous. I feel angry at the thought of them up there in my room together, doing whatever it is they're doing. Emma knows how I feel about him and I'm pretty sure she would never make a move because of it, but with me not sure what I want with the guy, and her being as into guys as she is, maybe there is something going on that I've been too blind to see.

Is it happening all over again? Is this where I kiss him, put myself on the line only to be pushed away because he doesn't feel the same? Could I really be recreating my past instead of starting over the way I want? Could Emma be the one that Graham wants and all of this is just a game to the both of them?

I'm going to drive myself crazy thinking like this. Graham has never done anything to hurt me before, at least not intentionally. If he knows how I'm feeling since Ryan died, there is no way he would play a game with me. It's not in him to be that way. I need to trust him and push this jealousy down.

It's hard to do though because I love him. I've always loved him. That's what asking him to stay was all about. If Ryan is gone, taking with him the powerful connection the two of us shared, then it's time that I admit that the only other person that could own my heart is Graham. He owned it in the beginning and maybe now, this is our chance for him to own it forever.

That is if I'm not too late and he's already moved on.

God, I want to go back in there, climb the steps, force my way into the room and confront both of them. I want to slap him and tear her eyes out for even looking at him. They can't be together, it's just not right because Graham, he's mine.

"Ser?"

Crap. So much for going under the radar.

"Hey..."

"Why aren't you in class?"

"Um, didn't want to be there?"

"Why are you answering my question with a question?"

"Because I don't wanna admit the real reason I'm here."

He smiles and despite my worry over what he was doing up in my room for so long, my insides turn to liquid at the sight of it.

"You miss me that much, huh?"

"Yeah, in your dreams maybe."

"It's about time a dream came true." He says, all traces of the smile gone and his expression as serious as his tone.

"What does that mean?"

"It means I want you to miss me that much. I want you to need me. It means you being here now, it's my dream coming to life."

"Dramatic much, Hudson?"

"Richards, why you continue to call me by my last name I'll never know, but yes, it's dramatic and it's also true. I didn't wanna leave you in class. I wanted to stay with you but I had to do this more."

"Do what exactly?" I ask but before he can answer, I add more to it. I need answers and I need them now before my mind runs anymore wild then it already has in the last twenty minutes since I saw him disappear behind my door. "And what does it have to do with Emma?"

"I could tell you that, but I think right now it would be better if I just show you."

"Show me what?"

"You'll see, if you agree to come with me."

"I'll go anywhere with you Graham, but what does that have to do with Emma?"

"I needed her help."

"With what?"

"A new beginning."

Chapter Thirteen

Going All In

Graham

After Emma called the community center, finding out as much as humanly possible about the dance classes and when they were running, there wasn't anything left for me to do but wait until class let out so I could meet up with Serenity again. I could have easily hung around the room for the duration, but the shaky way that Emma was on her feet proved to me that she needed to be back in bed and I needed to put the rest of the plan in motion.

Promising her again before leaving that what I was here to do for Serenity was the real deal and not some way of repeating my past mistakes; I left the dorm happier than I've been in a long time. Everything was coming together the way I wanted it to for the first time in years and the anticipation I had was hard to hide.

All the times we hung out together; going to parties, dances, hanging out in each other's rooms, never once did we ever do something like what I'm about to do with her now. We never did anything that felt like a date. The closest we came was the dance she asked me to take her to and while I looked at her in more than a friendly way that night, there was no way of knowing at the time that she did too, which is why this time it's different.

Dance classes might not be her thing, but it's a way for me to get closer to her without the pressure that would come from attempting to do it randomly on my own. I could wrap my arms around her, spin her around the room, dip her, maybe even kiss her and it would be the most natural thing in the world.

I'm not the most confidant person when it comes to making moves on girls. She's honestly the only girl I've ever wanted to experience anything with. I went on a few dates after she moved away, but it never felt the way it does with Serenity and if time has taught me anything at all, it's that I don't think it ever will.

Coming out of the dorms, prepared to head back across campus, the last thing I expect to see is her sitting on the steps outside, staring into space. It's like without realizing it, she's given me everything I could ever want being here like this right now. She's read my mind, seen directly into my heart and brought some of the dreams I've had to life.

I can tell when I call out that I've startled her. It's also obvious she hadn't been expecting me to catch her waiting out here. I'm not sure what made her leave class and make her way over here, but I'm really glad she did.

It means that I don't have to waste time waiting around. I can put this new beginning I want to create in motion and hope she's ready to share it with me.

When we go back and forth in the playful way we always do, I notice a mood shift when she brings up Emma and despite hating that she thinks there's something going on between me and her roommate, I can't help feeling my chest expand and my heart speed up knowing she's jealous and for some reason I don't get, that makes me happy.

"Are you going to tell me where you're talking me?" she asks as I lock my fingers in hers and pull her close to me, both of us walking slowly toward the parking lot and the car that will take us to our first destination.

"Nope. I want to show you. I've always been more about show than tell, Ser Bear."

"And I've always hated surprises."

"You're gonna like this one. Don't overthink it."

"Easy for you to say."

That's not true at all and I'm not gonna let her spend another second believing it. "Nothing about this is easy for me

Serenity. I don't have a clue what I'm doing. This is all new to me, same as it is for you."

"If it's not easy, than why do it at all?"

"Two years ago I had this chance and instead of taking it, I let it pass me by. I made myself a promise that if it ever came around again, I wouldn't make the same mistake."

She blushes and her hands come up in an effort to block it, something I'm not going to allow. Pulling her hand away from her face, getting a full view of the pink tinge to her cheeks, how natural it looks, threatens to completely undo me.

I am so fucking in love with this girl.

"Come on, we need to make a quick stop before I show you where I'm taking you."

I have no idea what's gonna happen next, if she's going to enjoy what I've got planned for us or if it's just going to make the real pain she's been going through even worse, but I do know one thing for sure.

I love her and I'm going all in.

Serenity

When Graham said he had a stop to make, the last place I expect him to pull into is a grocery store. I suppose I should expect this with him considering he's never been like every other person around him, but a grocery store?

I've been doing my best not to overthink what's happening, but it's a whole lot harder than I expect it to be. All I want to do is pull this apart piece by piece until I can figure out exactly what it is Graham is doing and what it means for us.

There's this part of me, knowing that he's taking me somewhere alone that thinks this is what dating him would feel like. I want to think of this as a date even though I'm still conflicted inside. Just as easily as I picture the two of us dating, it twists around until I see Ryan's face again and what our life was supposed to like after we made it out of the church.

What I don't feel any more is guilt. Being here in Graham's car while he drives me to parts unknown, I should feel guilty. A week ago I would have, but right now, it's the last thing I feel. I'm not sure Ryan would have wanted me to end up with Graham in the end, but I do know he loved me and would want me happy. Right now, I'm as close to happy as I can get.

I'm just not sure how long that happiness can last.

"We're here."

Looking out I take in where here is and I realize that I know this place. I've been here before. It hasn't been recently because with the weight of the world literally on my shoulders, I didn't have much time to go sightseeing, but I've spent time here before.

Tucker's Pond.

The first thing I did when I arrived in Stephenville was go sightseeing around the college. I'm not a fan of moving to a place and not knowing my way around; so I set out with no real destination in mind to get to know the area around me.

I came across a lot of different places that day, but this one, it had everything I could ever want. Not only is it peaceful, quiet with only the rustling of trees in the distance, but it also has the most scenic view I have ever come across.

The same way it was that day over a year ago, it is today as there's only the bare trace of movement across the water as the wind lightly blows around it and there again are a family of ducks, gliding along, looking as though they don't have a care in the world.

"You wanted to bring me to Tucker's Pond?"

"Yeah. When I went to talk to Emma earlier, I asked about places in town I could take you that wouldn't be filled with people. The movie thing, it's overdone and I wanted something more our style."

"What is our style exactly?"

"Quiet, away from the world and peaceful. Ser, I wanted to bring you to the one place that reminded me most of you."

"The pond reminds you of me?"

"Yeah."

"I don't know what to say to that." I answer honestly, his response catching me off guard. What he said is almost too sweet for words.

"Then don't say anything at all. Just come enjoy it with me."

"You should know—I've been here before."

"I sort of figured that. You did the same thing in Green Haven when you moved in."

"How did you know that?"

"Ser, you saw how I was the day I noticed you moving in. You really think I would just walk away that day and not try again?"

Honestly, I didn't give it a whole lot of thought before now. The day I met Graham was awkward because he happened to walk up when I'd been in the middle of an irritating conversation with a persistent spirit and I'd been more concerned with covering my own ass and not appearing weird than I was anything else.

Knowing now that he watched me after that, it's surprising. Until I started school a couple of days after that first meeting, I had no idea he even remembered I existed.

"I saw you one day when I was riding my bike back from the corner store. You were just walking along, taking everything in. You ended up at the park, sitting under the tree, looking up at the sky, but you went to a bunch of different places before that. It makes sense that you did the same thing when you got here."

"I like to know the places around me. It makes me feel safe."

"There's nothing wrong with it, but ending up at the park that day, it's the same thing as ending up here. The park in Green Haven reminds me of you the same way this place does. It's serene here. Calm. It's like the perfect place for you."

Serene. Wordplay on my name. Something I'm not used to and have no idea how to respond to. I suck at this stuff. I did with Ryan and I do now with Graham. He might have admitted that he has no idea what he's doing back at the dorm, but I've got him beat because I don't even know how to talk, much less know what to do right now.

"Since you've been here, it means you get to show me around."

We exit the car and make our way across the grass toward the water, all the while keeping our eyes locked on the ducks swimming along in front of us. I can't help thinking the closer we get to the edge of the water how right he is. This is serene and exactly what I need. It's my escape from the reality waiting for me back at school.

As always, Graham seems to know what I need better than I do.

"Where are you taking me?" he asks lightly and pointing out about five feet in front of us I show him. Just on the other side of the pond there's a dock, the perfect place to sit and take it all in without disturbing anything.

The first time I came here, I didn't even realize it was there and going as close as I could to the water, I ended up scaring the family of ducks and after watching them start to scatter, I looked up, saw the dock and the rest is history. I wasn't in the mood to repeat the same mistake twice.

I didn't want anything to ruin the moment right now. It was as perfect as it can be with the way my life goes.

The minute we're situated on the dock, our legs hanging out over the side, his hand again placed in mine, he breaks the silence by speaking.

"I'm really glad I did this."

"I'm glad you did it too." I reply truthfully. You never know how much you need something until you're put in a position of having it. I don't know why I didn't think of doing this sooner. Maybe the rough edges around my heart would have been healed a whole lot faster if I had just come out here in the first place.

This is my version of heaven or at least what I want it to be. Having actually been there, knowing the way even thinking of it makes me feel, it's nowhere near what this is for me. This is the end I want right here.

"What are you thinking about?"

"How perfect this is."

"The pond or the company?" he asks and as I look up I catch the smirk and smack him lightly.

"Both, but nice attempt at fishing for a compliment, Graham Cracker."

"Gotta take them where I can get them."

As we both laugh, I take in the sound. I'm enjoying the sound of our laughter mixing together. It's like our own personal music.

"So back at the dorm you said you wanted this to be a new beginning. What did you mean by that?"

"You sure you wanna know?"

"Normally, when someone asks a question, it's because they wanna know the answer, Graham." He catches my smile and laughs lightly before letting his eyes fall down to where our hands are resting together.

It's just like old times with him. He's easy to read and he doesn't even have to say a word. This isn't about a fresh start for us individually, it's his attempt at a new beginning for us together. To do away with the past and start over.

"Serenity, you know how I feel about you. I think deep down you've always known, the same way I've always known but never admitted to knowing how you felt about me. I spent a whole lot of time not believing in it, thinking that I was just reading into the way you were with me. I don't want to do that anymore. I want to be with you."

His eyes right now. God, they're turning me inside out. When I kissed him last night and I was able to catch a small glimpse of the way he looked, his eyes were a deep green, fueled by what I can only believe to be desire for me, but now they're the complete opposite. They're softer, tender and where they had been dark the night before, they're lighter now.

"You want to be with me?" I repeat in an attempt to make them seem more real. Gauge my own reaction to it and if the fullness I'm feeling in my chest is any indication, I already have my answer. I want the same thing that he wants, even though it scares the hell out of me.

"We've always been there for each other as best friends. There was a time where we both wanted more than that but were too afraid to go through with it. That's what I want now. What we had this morning when I woke up with your arm wrapped around me. Feeling you that close, the beat of your heart against my back. Your face being the first thing I see when I open my eyes. Falling asleep having you connected to me. Knowing you're safe there."

"Graham..."

"No, wait, don't say anything yet okay? Let me get all of this out."

"Okay."

"You said this morning that Ryan would want you to live. Well, I see it too but I see something more. I think Ryan would want you to be with me because I know everything there is to know about you, about who and what you are and it only makes me love you more. You're not the only one that wants to honor him here, Ser. I do too. I want to be your safe place to fall, the person you come to when you can't fight anymore and I want to do the fighting for you. I want to be the keeper of your secrets and the person that makes all your dreams come true. I want my version of heaven. I want you."

This is the second time he's called me his heaven and it doesn't get easier to hear no matter how many times it's repeated. Knowing that's how he sees me, it's overpowering, intense and scary all at the same time. It's also beautiful, perfect and a total Graham thing to say.

He might be a guy, but he's one of the most honest guys I know and when he says he feels something or believes something to be a certain way, he means it. He's secure in everything he feels and even though it might take him a lot of time to get the words right, there's no doubt that he's authentic when he finally does say them.

What he doesn't know is that everything he wants to be for me, what he wants with me, I want too and I know beyond a shadow of a doubt that Ryan would want it to be Graham that it happens with too.

It's what my dreams this morning were trying to tell me. What I had with Ryan wasn't meant to last forever. It shouldn't have even happened at all if what the angels told me has any truth to it. It means that what we shared, as short as it was, was leading me to this moment right here, sitting on this dock with Graham.

Ryan McGregor was brought into my life to bring me to this point and for the first time in a really long time, I'm going to listen to what I'm being shown and do what I should have done a long time ago.

"Are you finished?"

"Yeah, I guess I am."

He's nervous now, unsure of what it is I'm about to say to him now that I know he's finished. The softness, it's still present in his eyes but there's an uncertainty there now that wasn't before he admitted everything. It's that look that drives me forward. It's time to tell him how I feel.

"Standing in that church, believing that I wouldn't make my way out, my entire life flashed before my eyes. The good moments, the horrible ones, but more than all of that were the visions of things I would never get to experience before my life ended. Whenever my time to go is, I don't ever want to have things haunting me. Words left unsaid, feelings not felt, a life that wasn't lived to the fullest. I want to live my life like every day could be my last because tomorrow isn't a guarantee."

"What does that mean?"

"It means that we let the chance pass us by once before and I don't want to let it happen again. I don't want to live my life without knowing what it feels like to be loved by you and to love you just as deeply in return. Graham, I don't want to not take this chance and spend the rest of my life regretting it. I already spent the last two years doing that."

"Are you saying what I think you're saying?"

"Depends, I guess. What do you think I'm saying?"

I'm deliberately playing with him now. He has to know what I'm saying so his question is silly. He wants me to come right out and tell him that I want to be with him, and I will, but not before he does it first. We wouldn't be us if this was easy.

"It means that just like I thought, you're hot for me and can't deny it anymore. Your need to have me overpowers the urge inside you to fight."

Slapping him I laugh and it's a real genuine laugh, one that I've had so many times before with him but not recently. It makes it even more obvious that being with Graham is the right thing. It's what needs to happen. He's the only person alive that can make me feel like myself again.

"Yeah, that's it exactly!"

"Are you sure?"

"I've never been so sure. I want to do this, Graham. I want to be with you."

Chapter Fourteen

Cat and Mouse

Lucifer

It is time. Everything is exactly the way I need it to be in order to make this go off the way I imagine it. What I witnessed the day before has only deepened which makes my position that much stronger.

In order for this to work, Graham and Serenity must be as close as two people can get. It is only a matter of time before they consummate the love between them, but that matters little at this point. Them connecting again, the bond they share being ignited, that is all that is needed.

The final stage of my plan can now begin. I have used all the power afforded to me and have found that which I have been searching for since my supposed demise in Green Haven. I have found the perfect vessel. The very being I will use as a weapon in my war against Heaven and my father. The very being that will bring about the end of the world.

Ryan McGregor upon his release from Heaven and their attempts to save the human buried deep inside had been sent to Purgatory, though he had not been easy to find. After some time spent searching, sending my most trusted confidantes into the bowels of the place in order to gain information, he has been located and is here with me now, preparing as I am to make his reentrance.

Bringing him back is not an easy task. I cannot just possess him the way I would an average being. Because of the demonic part of him, I must use not only the old power I have acquired since my descent from Heaven, but also that of the most basic of magic. This possession will be different and will be done right.

As long as things were in a virtual upheaval, performing this act could not happen, but with the progression as far as Graham and Serenity are concerned, not to mention the silence from Heaven, there is no better time than now.

Situating myself before Ryan's lifeless form, closing my eyes and focusing all of the power and concentration into only him, I begin, starting first by chanting the words that will connect us and give me the one thing that I have been eagerly anticipating since putting the plan into motion to begin with.

Control.

"Transfer my soul into this vessel, let me not have to wrestle. Make it easy, make it fine and let his body become mine."

I speak the words repeatedly, feeling the energy in the darkened room shift as it begins to take effect. No longer am I standing before the lifeless form that seconds ago had been before me; instead I am one with him, feeling more alive than ever before.

Taking my first movements in my new vessel, I listen as his bones and muscles crack and strain under the weight of my power. Having not been active in weeks, his body will be in need of some fine tuning before I make my first appearance back at the college, but I have no doubt as I completely stand to my feet, moving him forward, working him in; that this plan will indeed go off without a hitch.

Not only is the demon still very much alive inside of him, but it is hungry. It wants revenge for the end it met and I am more than willing to give it to him.

When he had been alive, his revenge would have been targeted toward me, but now, with me being the one to control him, it will be focused on not one individual but an entire race of them.

Not only will I use Ryan to bring about Serenity's defection and eventual demise, but I will also destroy that of her soul-mate and guardians as well.

Yes. It is time. Everything has gone according to plan. I am now prepared again to bring the world and everything Heaven holds dear to its knees. I could not be more delighted if I tried.

Gabriel

Everything is not as it appears.

During my time watching over Serenity, albeit distanced so that she would be none the wiser about it, Michael called to me. Normally that alone would not have been enough to get my guard up as he has called on me numerous times before, but the urgency of the moment is made worse when I hear from my father minutes later.

Being home, the place where despite all that has happened still remains the most peaceful place in existence for me, I have hardened myself. Knowing what I do about Ryan now, what Father kept from us, as well as my part in informing the humans about it, it calls for me to take a different stance than I have in previous times standing before the man I envision as my father.

As I expect, his reason for calling me home and away from my charge has to do with Lucifer. What we spoke of the last time we came together has indeed picked up pace and turned into something far darker in nature. There is no doubt about what will take place now.

We are to prepare ourselves accordingly because again, just as we did a few weeks ago, we are about to go to war and this time, Father did not want us to lose.

"Lucifer has taken a vessel. It has been blocked from me, which as you know disturbs me to no end, but knowing your fallen brother the way I do, I believe we need to expect the unexpected."

"You believe that he has chosen someone close to Serenity, do you not?"

"Precisely. Michael has already been down and checked on the roommate. She appears to be exactly as she has always been. Blissfully unaware, which means it will not be her."

"Father, you are aware of the way Serenity has lived her life up until this point. There has not been many she has allowed herself to get close with. Other than Graham, who else could it be?"

"It is not the soul-mate. Possessing Graham has proven thus far to be difficult as he has not left her sight since the two of them connected. It leaves only her mother and a few acquaintances that she has made since her time at school."

"Do you really believe he would go to her mother? Knowing the strain between them?"

"Having the vessel blocked from me Gabriel, it makes it so I cannot discount anything. Their relationship may be strained but I have no doubt that if push came to shove, Serenity would protect the woman, even if it meant her own demise."

He has a lot more faith in Rachel Richards than I do. I have witnessed their relationship from the beginning and it has never been one spoken of in a pleasant way. As far as I have been able to tell, there is no relationship between them at all. Rachel has pushed her daughter away to a point where Serenity was forced to create her own family.

"I am sending you and Michael down to keep an eye on things. He is close to putting whatever plan he has in motion and I do not want any of you alone. Until I am able to figure out exactly what his end game is, you are to guard not only each other, but Serenity and Graham as well."

"Should we make them aware of all that is happening?" Michael asks, almost as if he is reading my mind. With Father still unaware that we had filled them in about Ryan, asking this is a calculated risk and one that I hope does not tip him off any more than he may already be.

"It would be in their best interests to also be on guard about this, so yes. Go to them and make them aware. Inform the Hudson boy that he is not to leave her side for any reason. Doing so could spell disaster and after what Lucifer has already managed to get away with, I will not let him do any more."

It is time for us to take our leave. As we both turn to go, believing the conversation to be over, Father calls to me, freezing me in place.

"Michael, I need a few moments with Gabriel. Please do as I have asked and wait for him. He will be along shortly."

With only a nod in response, Michael disappears and we are left on our own. What he needs to speak with me alone about, I cannot be sure but I have suspicions and all of them point to what we had done in going against him.

"I am aware of the power used in order to cloak yourselves from me. What I do not understand is why you did it in the first place."

"They deserved to know the truth and it seems as though you are more preoccupied with Lucifer than making sure that your ball of light knows what she is truly up against."

"Did informing her of Ryan work out well for either of you?"

"No, but we did not expect it too. All of us are guilty for what happened to the boy and it is no surprise that she agrees. If anything it brought her closer to Graham, which in the end is what you also want; is it not?"

"Why would you ask me that?"

"Father, it is no secret that in the end she will make her way back here and take her rightful place in Heaven. It is also no secret that in order for her to do that, she must again be joined with her soul-mate. You will be the one needed to bring them back together in that way again."

"I am well aware of what is needed."

"Then why even ask me that question at all?"

"I wish to know how you found out what the end result would be since I have not thought about it in your presence, nor have I spoken aloud of it."

"It is just a matter of putting everything together. No one needs to speak of it. It is just fact. I am more interested as to why you are not as angry as I expected you to be."

"You are not the only one that put together what they already knew in order to come to a certain result."

"You did the right thing, Gabriel. She did need to know what was going on, what we had learned and it has nothing at all to do with the soul-mate and bringing the two of them back together. She loved the man she believed to be a half demon. She saw in him what we were oblivious too because of his past history and allegiances."

"Yes; she did and it saddens me that we did not listen to her sooner."

"Do you recall the conversation we had a few months before the undertaking began?" he asks and it takes me off guard. It was such a long time ago and at the time I believed he hadn't heard any of what I had been trying to tell him. Now though, it appears I was wrong. He heard far more than I first thought.

"Yes of course."

"I do believe that if Serenity is successful in defeating Lucifer and is called home, it will be time for me to put more responsibility in your hands."

"What does that mean?"

"It means that when you both come home and Serenity has been made whole again, I would like you to work with me. It is time that Heaven as you say, has an overhaul. We need to start operating differently if we want the peace to remain in place."

I cannot believe what I am hearing. There was a time when I believed he had lost faith in me completely. To see him standing here, putting all of his faith and trust in my words from so very long ago, it fills me with a sense of pride I have never had before.

"In order for that to happen, we need to figure out Lucifer's plan. Once we have done that and Serenity is in the position to defeat him, then we can focus on making both Heaven and Earth a better place."

"Very well Gabriel. Take your leave now, meet up with Michael. I would like to get ahead of this. We cannot repeat past mistakes."

"No we cannot. We will keep you abreast of everything we learn."

As I separate from him, appearing in front of Michael as he stands watch over the dorm where Serenity and Graham are locked away safely for the evening, I take in everything that happened, debating whether or not to tell my brother of all that was shared between us.

Michael has always been Father's chosen one. He has been the one to stand beside him after Lucifer had fallen. Hearing that once the undertaking had reached its end and we were sent home again, things would be changing, it keeps me silent. Michael treasures his position with Father more than anything in the world. The last thing that I need is to say the wrong thing and have it all blow up in my face.

I would tell Michael the truth, but not yet. First, we had to make sure we stopped our fallen brother before he succeeded with an undertaking of his own.

Serenity's life depended on it.

Chapter Fifteen

The Wait is Over

Serenity

Two things happened when I woke up this morning and I'm not quite sure how to deal with either of them.

There wasn't anything particularly mind blowing about the way I woke up. I was in my bed like always and I turned over just like every other time, but this is where things start to get a little crazy. Turning over, I don't see the wall the way I usually do. I see something that resembles a wall of course, but only because of the hardness of his chest. Past that, there is nothing at all about Graham Hudson being in my bed that reminds of any other morning before this one.

If being there wasn't enough, the smile I receive the minute my eyes lock on his, is enough to turn my brain to complete mush. It's seeing him this way, having him near that brings about the first instance that I'm not quite sure how to handle.

Up until this moment, I've only ever cared for one other person, loved one other person and we didn't get a chance to be anything to each other than an answer to prayer. So what that means is, this is the first time I've ever been someone's girlfriend and it scares the living shit out of me. I can barely handle when someone attempts to flirt with me. How I'm going to handle being someone's other half is completely out of my realm.

I need Emma. That's what comes to mind first. She's dated before, even though after Cody she seems to have kept to hanging out with a bunch of random guys instead of just sticking close to one. She will know how to be a girlfriend. She's going to be able to tell me tons of things that will help me adapt to this so I don't screw it up five minutes after it happens and send Graham running.

If that wasn't enough on its own, I'm also dealing with how close we really are. What I experience when we're in bed this way together, even though we're not doing anything but cuddling. It's what our bodies experience that I'm so unfamiliar with. I've taken classes and been around enough girls to know how everything works, but to actually say I've been with someone in the most primal of ways, it's another gigantic red mark on my life as far as relationships go.

Before I turned to face him this morning, I felt him. He was pressed up against my back and there could be no mistaking his arousal. It's completely natural, every guy on the planet deals with it, but this; it's never happened in direct correlation to me before. He's reacting to me, the way my body scoots back into his, rubbing up against him. I'm doing things to him without even trying and it scares me.

Now that I've admitted to him that I want to take a chance and be with him the way we should have been years ago, is he going to expect things to progress to the point where we're together in the most intimate of ways or is he just as confused by all of this as I am so it's the last thing on his mind?

Do I even bring this up or bury it the way I've been doing since I woke up?

God, I hate being a girl. I hate being an inexperienced girl even more. Most girls have gotten past this awkwardness by now. College is supposed to be the time where most girls break away from the mistakes they made in high school, sleeping with boys they didn't really love or what not, and branching out and trying new things. I didn't have that and now I'm left feeling like I'm fifteen all over again.

This is what I do know. If there is anyone on this planet that I want to be with, after everything that's happened, it's Graham. I know that I want him to be my first. In fact, I'm pretty sure I want even more than that. I don't want him to just be the first boy I give myself to. I want him to be the only one.

The first and last. Who better to experience your first time with than the other half of your soul?

"Someone's thinking too much."

"That obvious?" I awkwardly laugh, downplaying the fact that he's right and I am thinking way too much for my own good.

"Hmm, yes. Definitely obvious when your body goes from being relaxed to tense in ten seconds or less."

"I'm sorry."

"Don't be sorry, Ser. Just tell me what's going on up there." He asks, rubbing his finger softly across my forehead, causing my body to shiver in response.

It's always been this way with him. Sometimes it's just a shiver, other times it's more than that. My body feels hot, I can feel sweat rising to the surface and my heartbeat rises until it's racing both in my head and my chest. Graham has no idea that one simple touch from him is enough to drive me wild, another thing that's so new to me I don't know what to do with it.

"It's not important. Just girl stuff."

"I like girl stuff. How about you tell me all about it while I braid your hair and paint your nails. I've been dying for a girl's night anyway."

I slide the pillow out from underneath me and swat him with it, laughing as he catches it easily and turns it around on me.

"I was wondering if I could make you laugh."

"You always do."

"So, you gonna tell me what's going on in that pretty head of yours or keep me guessing?"

I've got a choice now. I can tell him everything I'm thinking even though it's awkward and silly, or I can keep it to myself, driving myself crazy for the rest of the day as I try to make sense of it. Since it has to do with him, there's no other person besides Emma I would ever talk with about it, but it still doesn't make me eager to do it.

"Promise you won't laugh?"

"I can't promise that. Laughing at you brings me so much enjoyment."

As I attempt to swat at him again and he ducks his head, both of us breaking out in laughter in the process, I make my decision. I'm going to tell him everything and hope to god it doesn't send him running.

"I'm thinking about us."

"What about us?"

"Being together, dating, what it all means."

"Okay. I get the feeling there's more that you're not saying, so you wanna make things easy and just break it down?"

"This morning—uh, when I woke up, you were pressed against my back and I felt—"

"Oh!" he says, the light bulb going off, a look of understanding crossing his face as his eyes go soft. "Ser, I'm sorry. I had no idea—that was happening."

He's blushing now and for the first time since I woke up and my mind went into overdrive I feel like I did the right thing telling him everything. He's just as awkward at all of this as I am, which means I'm not going through this alone the way I thought. He gets it.

"I know. I wasn't bothered by it. It was actually kind of nice, but you should know I've never been with anyone before."

"I haven't either. I always thought that when I did it for the first time, I would be doing it with you, so, um—yeah. I didn't want it to happen with someone random. It's supposed to mean more than that."

He's melting my heart and he doesn't even know it. Knowing that he wanted to wait for me, not wanting to be with anyone else even though being with me wasn't a guarantee until now, it's intense. The only thing I don't like about it is that I can't say the same thing back to him.

Ryan and the way I feel about him, it means I can't say with certainty that I would have waited for Graham. If he lived through what happened with Lucifer, there's no telling where we would have ended up and even just thinking about this with

Graham staring at me with his soft eyes and tousled bed ridden hair, looking beyond perfect tears me up inside.

I want to tell him that I'm the same way but I can't.

"Ser."

"Hmm?"

"You wanted to be with Ryan; didn't you?"

"No. I mean, I don't know. It never got that far. I know what I felt whenever we were together, but we never talked about it and I'm not exactly the most experienced with stuff like that."

"That makes two of us."

"I'm not sure I'm ready to take that step."

He goes silent and it hurts despite every attempt not to let it. I don't want him to think that because I'm not there yet that I won't ever be or that this has something to do with Ryan, because for once, this choice has nothing to do with the man I lost. It's what feels right for me.

"Do you remember what I said yesterday?" he asks softly and looking up, seeing his eyes staring intently back at me, I nod. "I said I would wait forever to be with you and at the time I meant dating, but it's the same for this too. If we're going to be together, it's going to be because both of us are ready."

A huge weight has been lifted off my shoulders hearing him say this. It means that for the time being, I don't have to overthink it. We can take our time and navigate all of this together. There's no rush. We'll find our way when the time is right. It's exactly what I need to hear.

He pulls me to him and gently brushes his lips across my forehead before dipping lower and kissing my nose and then my lips, lingering a split second longer than the other places, both of us just enjoying the way it feels.

"We've got all the time in the world, Ser." He whispers when he pulls away cuddling me closer to his body, wrapping me in his warmth and reminding me again why I fell in love with him in the first place. Knowing how my mind works, he just knows the right words to say all the time. The ones that will bring me the calm I so desperately need.

"Thank you for yesterday."

"You're welcome, but I should be the one thanking you."

"Why?"

"Because the dance class, it was a selfish move. I wanted to recreate the night we were together at the dance. I wanted to have my arms around you that way again and you delivered."

The dance. The stupid high school dance that I wanted to use as a way to break out of my shell more. The one I asked him to because I didn't want to go alone, but also because I liked him and wanted to experience the very same thing he's talking about now.

"You're not the only one that was selfish."

"Well, now you've got my attention. When were you selfish?" he whispers into the back of my hair, sending shivers down my spine with the way his breath feels on my bare shoulders.

"Asking you to the dance, it wasn't because you were my best friend. It was because I wanted to have your arms around me while we danced."

He kisses the back of my neck, right where it meets my shoulders and there's just something so intimate about it that I freeze. I'm pretty sure he has no idea he's doing it, but kissing me there, right in that exact spot, it's turning me on. It's an experience that's only happened for me one time before and it brings the memories flooding back which just causes me to flinch in pain.

"Trust me. If this was going to lead to where your mind imagines, there most definitely would not be an audience. For a very long time."

I don't want to remember this now. It's not right.

"Where did you go just now?" he asks and I shake my head in response. I can't tell him this. With as good as everything has been this morning, there's no way I'm dropping this and turning it sour. I need to keep this to myself.

The problem is, with Graham; that won't ever happen.

"Memories."

"Okay. Something I said or something I did?"

"Something you did, but Graham..."

"You don't have to explain. It will get easier. We just take our time until the only memories you have are good ones."

Damnit. Graham Hudson is the most incredible person I've ever known.

"We should get going anyway, unless you're planning on ditching Psych again?"

"Definitely not. You have no idea what he's like with people who ditch or show up late. You should ask Emma sometime."

As we both move around in the bed, sitting up before sliding out, one after the other, still managing to find ways to touch throughout, he turns back to me when he's standing, giving me a full view of his bare chest, a way I've never seen him before now. The heat I experienced when he kissed the back of my neck earlier is magnified and it takes every bit of restraint I have not to reach out and pull him back down onto the bed with me.

Maybe we won't be waiting so long after all. If seeing him shirtless is enough to drive me completely crazy, I can only imagine what seeing him completely naked will do.

"You alright?" he says, breaking through my not so innocent thoughts and back to reality and the very real class we need to get to.

"Perfect." I answer back easily and as he slips my hand in his and heads for the door, I realize just how true that is. For the first time in weeks, I really do feel pretty damn close to perfect and it's all because of him.

Graham

People always tell you to expect the unexpected. In doing so, nothing can ever take you by surprise because you'll always be waiting for it just around the bend. I've never done that. I don't go into experiences in my life on guard for the change.

Today might be a good time to change that.

When we finally make our way out of her room and across campus, and into Psych class, one of those expect the unexpected moments hits me right between the eyes.

Sitting in his seat, owning it like he never even left is Ryan.

It's obvious from the way she just keeps making her way up the aisle that she hasn't seen him yet, but there's no mistaking that I have. I'm making it so hard on her, holding her hand the way I am yet barely moving that she finally turns around to face me and that's when it happens.

She catches my line of sight and follows it. Her eyes land on Ryan and if I thought my stance was frigid, thrown off by what I'm seeing, she's even worse. Serenity's body, it sags into mine just the way I'm expecting it too. Seeing Ryan sitting there with a smile plastered across his face, it's too much for her to take.

What kind of sick joke is this? Didn't Gabriel and Michael say he couldn't be saved? That in dying the way he did in Green Haven he ceased to exist based on what he truly was underneath?

If all of that is true, then how the hell is he sitting here right now, his eyes locked on the two of us, still smiling like he didn't just spend the last month away from her?

"Am I dreaming?" she whispers into me and I shake my head in response. I don't even have the words for this right now. None of it makes sense.

"You wanna get out of here?"

Now it's her turn to shake her head. Seeing Ryan, it can't be easy. I'm having a hard enough time with it and we don't exactly have the history the two of them do. If she wanted to bail out of here right now, I wouldn't blame her. It actually hurts that she doesn't because it's all I wanna do. I need to get as far away from this as possible.

The minute we're seated, I expect the guy to say something, turn in our direction but none of that happens. Serenity turns her body around in her seat to level me with a look, but Ryan makes no motion to follow her. His eyes are firmly planted ahead and if I wasn't already so thrown off by the entire thing, I might question why.

Serenity and Ryan, they're married now. Gabriel told me that they went through with the wedding before the battle started, so shouldn't he be wanting face time with the woman he pledged to love until death do they part?

I suppose all bets are off when death actually does separate them.

"We need Gabriel." She admits and I nod in agreement. We do need the angels. It's the only way we can make sense of this, but it's not as if we can just call for them in a class that's full of students that have no idea who and what Serenity really is.

"Yeah, we do, but until we can get the hell out of here and call them, we're gonna have to deal with it." I whisper back, not wanting the guy we're talking about to hear us. "How are you handling this?"

"I'm not sure it's even real, so I guess better than expected."

That makes two of us. I think seeing him here, it's thrown us both for a loop so we're just going through the motions, believing that we're still somehow in her dorm asleep because the reality is too heavy to handle.

"Do you think I should say something?" she asks and I shrug. I have no idea what she should do in this situation. I didn't even think this was possible.

"I'm gonna do it. It's not like I can just sit here and not acknowledge him." She says, more to herself than to me and when she turns her body straight ahead, I watch as her eyes seem to take him in.

I hate that this is happening. That right now the girl I pledged my love to less than twenty-four hours ago is again focusing her attention on another guy. I know I need to trust her, but with him back and how easily she's gone to him before, I can't help feeling that what happened before is taking place all over again.

I'm gonna lose her before I've had the chance to really have her.

"Ryan?"

He turns his head toward her and the smile is still there, only this time it's reaching straight into his eyes like he's happy to see her and it just twists the knife in my gut that much more.

"I was wondering when you were gonna acknowledge my existence."

Damn that smile. I wanna knock it off his face and I'm not a violent person. He doesn't get to disappear for weeks and come back flashing it at her and get whatever he wants. Does he have any clue the shit he put her through? The shit I'm still working to fix?

There's one silver lining here though. Where I expect Serenity to react to him the way she did when she first caught sight of him, it appears as though she's not. She's suspicious of him and her next words only confirm it.

"So, where have you been?"

"Healing. When Heaven dumped me off, I wasn't as dead as they thought."

His answer is too quick, like it's been rehearsed. I would bet every dime I have that he wasn't off healing the way he says. There's definitely something more going on here. The way she softens with his response though, it's clear she doesn't feel the same.

Shit Serenity; don't fall for this. He's playing you.

Knowing she can speak to the dead, I want her to be able to hear my thoughts now with as strongly as I'm thinking them. I want her to be as guarded as she was when we first sat down, when she asked him where he's been. I don't think my heart or my head can take her changing things up and gravitating toward him again.

"Michael seemed pretty sure."

"Yeah, well you know how they felt about us together, pretty girl. Doesn't it make sense that they would say whatever worked to get what they wanted?"

"You really believe that?"

"I do. They wanted to keep us apart even before everything went down. It makes sense that they'd want it still."

Shit. She's buying into this bullshit, I can see it all over her face. Her eyes are soft and her body is lax, something that since I came back days ago, she's only done with me.

"Ser..." I speak up, not wanting this to go on any longer than it already has. I can make out the professor at the front of the room, ready to start the class and it's as good a time as any to break this up before he says anything else that will pull her in.

Turning her body to me, she smiles weakly, silently telling me something but it's not something I easily understand. Is the smile her way of telling me that I have nothing to worry about or is there more to it?

"Be careful." Is all I can manage, turning away from her and focusing on the front of the class. I want to say so much more than that but with the half demon sitting across from me, listening in on every word I'm saying, I need to be careful. The less he knows about how I feel about this situation the better.

"I will." She whispers, reaching out and running her fingers across my hand. As always, the contact between us, it turns all rational thought I might have been having to crap and all I can focus on is the sharp tingle that's now making its way up my arm and down through the rest of my body.

"Serenity, I know all of this doesn't make much sense, but uh, after class, I'd really like to go somewhere and talk to you about it. There's so much I need to tell you."

Over my dead body he's taking her anywhere alone. If he wants to explain what the hell he's doing here and what his game is then he can do it with me right there by her side or not at all. She may believe the shit he's spouting off right now, but I didn't and I don't care how much of an over protective asshole that makes me.

I need to keep her safe until we can both sit down and talk with Gabriel about this. He would know what the hell is going on and be able to stop whatever it is before it begins.

It's when she speaks again that I realize what I want and what is going to happen are two separate things. She's taking the choice away from me and in typical Serenity fashion, she's putting herself on the line again.

"Yeah, we do need to talk."

"So after class, will you come with me?"

"Yeah, Ry; I'll come with you."

Just when I think I've lost her completely, she turns around in her seat again and levels me with a smile. Holding out a small slip of paper in front of her, her body turned so that Ryan won't be able to make out what's happening, she slips it into my hand before turning around again.

It's only when I look down and read the words inside that my heart settles. She's not buying into this at all. She's just doing what needs to be done in order to get answers.

When we get out of class, I'm going to go with him. Call Gabriel, tell him what's going on. I'll meet you in my room when it's over. Don't worry Graham Cracker, I'll be fine. <3

Chapter Sixteen

Forever Until The End

Serenity

Three weeks ago, coming back to school, walking the grounds, hiding away in my room, I prayed for this moment to happen. To wake up one day, go to class and see him sitting there in his seat, smile firmly implanted on his face, eyes only for me. I craved it because the agony I felt knowing I lost him was almost too much to bear.

It's happening now the way I wanted it to then, but I don't feel the same and it has nothing to do with Graham and everything we've admitted to each other over the last few days.

I don't feel the same because there's something not right about this. The angels haven't always been the most forthcoming with me, but I remember the agony Michael felt when he had to tell me that the man I loved was lost. I also remember the way Gabriel came to me, night after night, his heart hurting the same way as mine because he couldn't give me back the one thing I wanted more than anything.

Those experiences, they aren't fake. They are very real and they aren't part of some angelic performance for my benefit, so as happy as I am that Ryan is sitting here now, I don't trust it enough to throw myself completely back into it.

We do need to talk and I do need to hear what he has to say because I think with all the changes I've gone through over the last month or so, I'll be able to sense deception from him. It wasn't all that long ago that he was shrouded in darkness, not only to me but to Heaven as well and I need to know before I put myself back out there if it's happening again.

Lucifer not dying the way we all thought, that's another reason none of this feels right. There's nothing stopping the fallen angel from using whatever means necessary to get to me again and there really is no better way than to use my own heart against me. It is the one thing that I consider a flaw now that I know I'm something more than just human. It's the only real human part of me left and it can be used and manipulated.

I can't let him do that if that is what's going on here.

I agreed to spend time with him after class because I know getting him alone, I'll be able to think clearly, see things from a different angle and get to the bottom of this. If Graham is with me, I'm going to focus on him, what's happening between us and less on the real issue we're facing. What he thinks, feels and experiences, they matter to me. They've always mattered to me, but I can't put that first right now.

He needs to be the one to go to Gabriel and Michael and let them know what's going on. I'm still damaged from everything they kept a secret and it makes any interaction I do have with them harsh at best. Graham, while on my side and understanding doesn't have the same problem and I know there's no one better to speak for me than him.

The way my body turns to his when he speaks, the way his smile makes my heart jump, it's all there as strong as it ever was and even though I'm with Graham now and I don't have any plans of backing away, it tears me up inside knowing that I'm reacting this way. It's not fair.

All of this thinking, it's driving me crazy. I can feel Graham's eyes even though I refuse to turn around and acknowledge them and I can also feel Ryan's. I'm caught in this tug of war, or at least my heart is with these two men that despite it all, I can't seem to let go of.

"Are you ready?" Ryan asks as he slips from his seat. "I thought we could grab some coffee and hang out in the quad again."

"Yeah, I'll meet you outside. Just wanna talk to Graham for a sec." I mumble off before turning to the other man in the equation in order to gauge his reaction to everything that's happening.

Ryan nods and heads for the door, leaving us alone and the minute he's out of earshot I breathe a sigh of relief. I've got so much going on in my head right now, I'm thankful that at least the biggest cause of it is gone. It's like I'm finally able to be me again despite the knots I seem to be tied up in.

"Are you sure going off with him is the right move?"

"If you've got a better idea, please tell me. He wants to get coffee and spend time on the quad. As long as we're doing all of this in public, I don't think my safety is gonna be a problem. We need answers don't we?"

"Yeah we do." He says, sliding his hand into mine and beginning the short trek that will lead us out of the class and toward the very man we just escaped from. "It doesn't mean I have to like it."

"Graham..." I start but he puts his free hand up to stop me.

"I know, Ser. You don't have to say it."

"I love you."

I can tell by the way his green eyes light up before he looks down at me that he didn't expect me to say what I did. It's just the only thing that for me is left to say. He needs to be reminded right now especially that despite Ryan being here, I meant what I said to him. I love him and I wanna try this with him, even if it doesn't end up the way we both want it too.

"I love you more."

"You wish."

He laughs and my heart feels lighter. As stressful as all of this is for the both of us, him laughing this way means that it hasn't gone too far yet. We're still able to be here and be us and not let the events of today, no matter now crazy they are, break us apart.

"I don't wanna be bothered by this, Ser, but I know what he means to you. I know what him being back means even if there's more going on. I don't want to leave you with him, not even for a second and it's not because I'm afraid things will change. It's because I don't trust him."

"Well, that makes two of us. I don't like this either, but you're right. It doesn't change anything. You know how I feel about him, I won't ever lie to you about that, but this time, it's not like before. I just want answers."

"So, go get your answers." He says the minute we're outside the building and Ryan again comes into view. "If something doesn't feel right though, I want you to get away from him okay?"

"I promise," I say as I press my lips to his, bringing my body safely into his arms. "I'll come back the minute things feel weird. Well, weirder."

"I guess I'll see you later then."

He sounds hurt; the knowledge that we're about to separate from each other for the first time in days weighing heavily on him. I need to make sure that he knows there's no guessing to it. He will see me later because after I get the answers I want, there's nowhere else I wanna be than back with him.

"You will see me later, no guessing involved." I whisper before kissing his nose one final time before releasing my hand and turning to the face the other guy in my life.

As I start making my way down the stairs toward Ryan, I hear Graham call out one more time behind me and the words he says, they just propel me even more forward.

He loves me.

It's that love that's gonna get me through the next little while with Ryan and it's that love that's gonna make me get to the bottom of this once and for all. For the first time since Green Haven, I can see a silver lining and it's not me standing alone or even me standing with Ryan and the angels that I can see.

It's Graham and me, the way it should be.

Graham

I'm no good at this stuff.

I've been hanging out in Serenity's room for about a half hour now, her giving me her keys so I could have this conversation with Gabriel in private while Emma is in class. I've called to the angel in my head, but since that doesn't seem to be getting me anywhere and I'm starting to think I'm limited on time, I'm gonna have to do it out loud next.

Speaking to an angel, sending the prayer or whatever it is up to them out loud, there's just something so crazy about it that I'm not sure I've got it in me. If it wasn't so important and Serenity wasn't counting on me, I'm not even sure I'd do it at all.

It is important though, so I suck it up and start speaking, hoping the entire time that this time, whatever I'm about to say gets through and one of them appears to me so I can get this over with.

"You told us to call for you if something happened. Gabriel; Michael, whoever hears this, something's going on and I think you need to get your butts down here and deal with it."

It's not the nicest way to ask for help, but it's all I've got.

This is all new to me. Angels, demons, even the devil. Up until a few months ago all of it was just stories I'd heard growing up but never really paid much attention to. Now, it's all very real and I'm still trying to do everything I can to catch up with how fast it's being thrown at me.

Serenity might be a ball of light from Heaven, she might even be an angel when everything is over and done with, but I'm just me. Normal, human me and no matter how much I stand by and support her through all of these insane changes, nothing will ever change it. We're never going to be on the same page because I'll never understand exactly what she is even though her being an angel is the only thing out of all of this that makes any damn sense.

I start to wonder how she's making out in her attempt to get answers from Ryan, but before I can really give it a whole lot of thought, the lights start to flicker and I know I'm getting my response, even if it did take them too damn long to do it.

Where I expect it to be one of them, I get both and neither one of them looks all that pleased to see me, which means my call to them out loud really wasn't the best way to go.

"For once, I am thankful." Michael says the minute he touches down and when he doesn't seem to get the response he wants from me, since all I've got is confusion, he speaks again as Gabriel makes his appearance. "You came to terms with the error of your ways before I had to call attention to it."

"Well, next time, give me a heads up on proper angel calling protocol and I'll do better."

"No need to be a smart-ass Graham."

Ignoring Michael and turning my attention to the one angel I can actually stand, I get right down to the reason I called them to begin with.

"Ryan's back and I'm pretty sure you both know that; so I guess the reason I'm calling on you is because I wanna know how the hell that's even possible."

"Must we give you the answer when it's clear you already know it?"

"Michael," Gabriel pleads. "Now is not the time."

"Yeah, Mike. Now isn't the time."

"Graham, I ask that you not get him going. Once you go down this path with Michael, it will never end."

"Fine, but you mind telling me how a guy that should have ceased to exist is sitting in the quad with Serenity right now looking more alive than ever?"

"Michael is right with what he said. I think you already know the answer, but are just waiting for us to confirm it. Lucifer is the reason."

Well, that answers that but it still doesn't explain how even the fallen angel could have made Ryan appear again if he had already vanished into thin air.

"Lucifer is in possession of some very old power. He is capable of anything at this point which is why this newest development does not surprise either of us. I am unsure of how he made it happen, but it appears as though he is in control of Ryan again."

"Control how?"

"Possession of course."

"So you're telling me that I just let Serenity go off on her own with Lucifer?"

"It would appear that way, yes."

Well this doesn't make me feel good at all. It was bad enough knowing I was letting her walk into the lion's den going off with Ryan, but knowing that it's not even him but the fallen angel, makes everything even worse.

"The time for beating yourself up has long passed. There is no way you could have known that it was not Ryan."

Gabriel is doing his best to make me feel better but that's not about to happen. I knew something was off about the guy. I knew it the minute I saw him sitting in the damn class but instead of pushing harder, making her see it the way I did, I let her go off so that I could come back here. He could be taking her god knows where right now and I'd be powerless to stop it.

"They are in the quad. No harm has come to Serenity and I do believe that right now it will not. Lucifer is merely trying to get through to her."

"So, why don't you both go down there and stop him? That is what you're supposed to do, right?"

"Yes, in a sense but Serenity, she is going to learn things right now that could prove valuable in the fight against our fallen brother. Putting an end to that would do nothing but throw us even further behind him and his plans. We must let this play out."

"What happens if he kills her?"

"Lucifer is a lot of things, but stupid is not one of them. He would not execute a move as foolish as to take her out on a crowded college campus. He will wait until the timing is right."

"And we're just gonna let him do this?"

"Do you not see how valuable her time with him can be to us, human? She could garner all sorts of plans from him that we might not know otherwise. Serenity is made of Heaven, she is not the human girl you believe her to be. She will rise to the occasion should she need to and take him out."

As happy as I am that they answered my call, having Michael here and acting like I'm a moron about all of this, it's pissing me off. I wish that he hadn't shown up at all.

"Wishes don't always come true, Graham. I'm here because I need to be."

"Fine, but can you stop treating me like I don't know what the hell is going on? I know what Serenity is, I think I've known it longer than anyone else, but it doesn't mean I like having her out there alone and exposed with him!"

"None of us do, Graham, but this is the situation we have been dealt. We must move forward accordingly. If she does not return soon, we will make our presence known. Until then, we need to let this play out and see where it takes us."

That might be all well and good for them but it's not how I operate. I don't care if she's made of the light or not, she's still my girlfriend; the one girl that I can even remember feeling anything remotely good for my entire life. Protecting her, keeping her safe, it's all that matters.

"Soul-mate bonds, they never cease to amaze me. They make the people in possession of them lose complete rational thought."

"Sort of like the beloved bond, huh Mike?" I shoot back, no longer willing to take any more of his smart ass remarks at my expense. I'm thinking rationally even if these two believe otherwise. I'm thinking the way I always have.

"That way of thinking is what will cause your immediate end if you are not careful. You can believe us to be harsh all you want, but Serenity is fine. She has everything under control and it would run much smoother if you kept your own emotions in check as it pertains to her."

"Shut the bond off then? Turn off how I feel about her and just let her go through whatever hell Lucifer has planned?"

"That is not what Michael means at all. He is merely stating fact with you though his manner of doing so leaves something to be desired. The bond, the connection the two of you have, it's what is making you so erratic right now. We don't want you to shut it off, we just need you to see past it to the bigger picture."

"What's the bigger picture?"

"Serenity ending Lucifer's reign. That is still what you want, is it not?"

He had me there. It is what I want. I don't want her having to be the one to do it, but it's the hand we've been dealt. I just want it over with so that we can go on and live some kind of life that doesn't revolve around the end of the world. I just want whatever is left of this life to be spent with her and her alone.

"The love, it's enough to turn ones stomach." Michael laughs and before I can respond, Gabriel frowns at his brother, proving I'm not the only one annoyed by his actions.

"Michael; it was not all that long ago you walked the same road with your love for Faith. I believe it best that in this way, you keep your opinions to yourself."

Smiling, kind of impressed that the archangel seems to have my back, I watch as both Gabriel and Michael's light seems to dim at the exact same time. Where they had been bright when they got here, now they're dim to the point that it's almost becoming hard to tell if they're really angels at all.

'What's with the light guys?"

"We need to move and we need to do it now. The time for waiting is over. Lucifer, despite the way things have appeared seems to have broken through somehow."

"What does that mean?" I ask as they both move toward the door. There is no way they're going down there without me. If he is doing something to Serenity, I'm going to do whatever I can to stop it.

"It means that through the vessel he has managed to touch a part of Serenity and if we do not handle it she could be lost to us forever."

That's all I need to hear.

There is no way in hell Lucifer is taking her from me, not when I just got her back. That will happen over my dead body.

Lucifer

I was not sure I would be able to pull it off when I first came into contact with Serenity again, but the more time we spend together, I can see that this is working just the way I wanted from the start.

Despite her distrust, she cannot help the pull that she experiences whenever she is in direct contact with the vessel. Yes, Ryan had been the perfect choice for this. It is only a matter of time before she willingly comes to my side and helps me achieve all that I have only dreamed about up until this point.

"Why would Michael lie to me? What does he gain from that?"

"I don't know, pretty girl, but you can see me right? I'm here and I'm alive."

"None of this makes sense."

"How do you think I feel? I fought to come back to you and the minute I show up, I see you holding hands with Graham; like what happened between us—it didn't even matter."

She sighs and it takes all of my power not to smile at the sound. I rather like when she feels bad, it creates a hunger inside of me for her, something that until now I had not paid much attention to. Maybe before I dispose of her, I can partake of one taste. Surely I will have earned it when all of this is said and done.

"It matters, Ry. I just don't know what you want me to say. I thought you were dead. I spent weeks grieving; missing you, needing you, wanting nothing more than for you to come back. Michael said you died. It meant you weren't coming back."

"So moving on with Graham seemed like the right move?"

"Yeah, I guess it did. He came back here, fought like hell to get through to me. He even made me see that it was okay to feel the way I do about you. He never once told me to stop feeling it; He saved me."

How would Ryan react in this situation? Would he flinch as if being stabbed by her words or would he not react at all? During all of my time with the boy, I never could quite figure him out emotionally. Doing the only thing I can in the moment, I allow Ryan's body to sag in defeat.

Ryan feeling the way he did for her means he would be hurt by her words. It is that avenue I have to take now.

"What does that mean for us, Ser? I mean, we're married."

"Yeah, we are." She sighs again, lowering her eyes away from me. "I don't know what it means."

"Do you love me?"

It is a risk asking her this question. I am aware of her feelings for the soul mate, but I know somewhere deep inside her, she is still very much in love with the man sitting on the grass beside her. I need to know how much hold I still have so that I can proceed accordingly.

"Yes. It doesn't just shut off, at least it doesn't for me, but I can't turn my back on Graham. He was here, you weren't."

"I'm here now."

"It's not enough. I know what they told me, Ryan. You shouldn't even be here at all."

"You're right. I shouldn't, but I am. I'm not going anywhere again. When they left me to die, I fought like hell to come back to you. I didn't want things to end that way. I know none of this makes sense and that you've got the angel's words swimming around in your head, but you know me. I would never lie to you."

She's softening. She knows I speak the truth. Ryan would never lie to her. The thing she does not realize is that I would lie in order to get her to join me, but after that happens, I would be much the same as him. Once I achieve what is needed, she would get nothing but the truth from me. It is why deceiving her this way is so easy.

"You being back, I don't know what it means; what I'm supposed to feel, say or even do. I never thought I would see you again. I know you want me to say everything can go back to the way it was, but I don't know if it can. Ry—" she stops and despite not wanting to let her get to me, she does exactly that. I hate hearing her voice fade away, especially with the pure emotion in it. "I need time."

Time. We do not have time. It was supposed to go differently, this talk with her. I was to tell her what happened to me after she last saw me, which has not yet happened and then get her to admit her feelings, bringing her closer to the end result I so desperately want to reach. It is not supposed to go this way now.

I cannot give her time but I can make it appear as though I do. Maybe doing things that way, she will soften even more.

"Just tell me we can work through this, Ser. Tell me I'm not too late."

The moment of truth is upon us and judging from the tears beginning to build in the corner of her eyes, threatening to fall at any moment, it appears as though I am going to get the result I crave. She will bend to me.

"You're not too late."

Just as I reach out to her in an effort to bring her close to me, it happens. Two lights as well as the shadow of the human soul mate appear directly behind us. Being here now tells me everything I need to know. They are aware of the truth even though Serenity is not and they have come to put an end to it.

"Serenity, things are not as they appear and you need to come with us now before it's too late."

Chapter Seventeen

Decisions

Gabriel

In true Lucifer fashion, the minute we appear he makes himself scarce. That on its own should have been enough for her to believe what I was about to tell her next, but of course, he had already done the damage.

"There is something you need to know, Serenity."

"I already know, Gabe."

"No, I do not believe you do with what you said when we arrived."

Graham had heard her words just as Michael and I did and the look on his face, it's troubling. He is not sad the way I expected him to be, more like confused and if it was not of the utmost importance to let Serenity know just who she had just spoken too, I would handle it.

As it stands, there is obviously a lot that the two of them need to speak about.

"You saw him as well as I did, Gabriel! Ryan is back."

"No, Serenity. He is not back. Not the way that you wish him to be."

"So I wasn't just sitting here with him, having a normal conversation before you had to come and ruin it?"

"If it is Ryan as you believe, why would he run from us?" I want to go easy with her, but right now, easy is not going to work. "Ryan knows of me as well as Michael and Graham. There is no reason for him to run. You must put the way you feel about the boy behind you for a minute and think."

She falls silent and I know she is doing as I ask. It's only when Graham moves toward her and she backs away I realize that she is still not reaching the end that I need her to. She has no reason to move away from Graham and it disturbs me to no end that it is happening at all.

"Gee, Gabriel. Maybe he's running because of the lies you told about him, or maybe knowing about Graham and me, it's too much."

"Ser, even you know that's stupid. Sure, he might know about us, but shouldn't that make him fight harder for you?"

I want to be thankful for Graham, but with the rage I see flash in her eyes after he says that what she thinks is stupid, him talking is only making this situation worse.

"The both of you need to stop coddling the girl. She is one of the purest lights in existence. She needs to be made aware of the facts even though she refuses to acknowledge them because of her human temperament." Michael states as he moves toward Serenity, his face made of stone.

"What truth?"

"We have no idea how it is possible, but Lucifer has resurrected Ryan in order to possess him. He is doing so in an attempt to get closer to you. Father made us aware of it earlier and Graham confirmed it for us."

This should be enough for her to understand. It should change things and make her join with us, but with Serenity it seems as though nothing ever goes according to plan because she backs away, as if she cannot stand to be even in the same vicinity as us.

"Serenity, you must see that what we are telling you is the truth. I know that you wish nothing more than for Ryan to come back and be the way he once was, but that is not possible. You need to accept that and come with us now."

She shakes her head and something inside me dies at the sight. It may be related to our bond or it may just be that going against us, she is breaking my heart, but whatever the reason I wish for it to cease. I cannot take seeing her this way. Father had been right all along. All of this was going to make things worse.

There really is a line that one must not cross when dealing with a human; even one as blessed as Serenity. She has reached the point of no return. She has heard all that she can handle.

"I'm not going anywhere with you."

"Ser—don't be like this. Please come with us." Graham pleads and just as it did when she shook her head at me, my heart breaks again hearing the strained sound of his voice. There can be no doubt that he loves her just as much as I do and her turning against me, against all of us tears him apart the same.

"No, Graham. I know what you're trying to do and I love you for it, but I need to be alone. I'm not stupid. I know what you're saying is true. It's not my Ryan anymore, but it still doesn't make anything I'm feeling less valid."

"Well, let me go with you. I don't want you going off alone."

She shakes her head again and this time I move toward her. If she is unwilling to come with us, then I will take her by force. It is a way that I never wanted to act with her, but just like the day in Green Haven before she married Ryan, I want to rip her away from here and make sure she never has to return. It is for her own safety after all.

"Stay away from me Gabriel. I know what you're gonna do and right now you're all running under the radar. All it takes is one scream and I can bring down a world of hurt on you."

"Calling attention to beings that no one else can see only makes you look crazy, Serenity." Michael says, but there can be no mistaking the humor buried in his tone. He finds the entire thing funny, of which I do not agree.

"Fine. I can handle being labelled crazy if it keeps you all away from me." She turns toward Graham and even though she is running through a gamut of emotions, her eyes soften when they land on him. "I need some time alone. Please let me have it."

"Graham, you were right originally. You cannot let her go off alone. There is no telling what Lucifer will try with the knowledge we have now given her. When he deluded her into believing he was Ryan, things were easier, but now...there is no telling."

He struggles with what he needs to do next and when I think I've said enough to get him to agree with us, he proves me wrong, the same way his soul mate does every single time I interact with her.

"Do what you need to Serenity; just come back to me when you're done."

It pains me to watch what happens next. The way her lips curve up into a smile for him, both of them embracing so intimately. Despite my claims that I needed to bury the bond we share, it is becoming increasingly hard to do when faced with pictures such as this one now. Graham owns a part of her that despite what happens next I will never be able to touch and it makes me so livid I have to step away so that I do not cause the boy harm.

"Gabriel, I do believe you now understand the struggle I faced so very long ago."

"As always Michael, your opinion is not needed."

"Who is acting like a teenager now?"

Despite the way I feel inside, I remember times past and smile at him.

"That makes you the baby then. Finally."

As Serenity and Graham break apart and she turns from us, prepared to take her leave to places unknown, the boy turns to me and all anger I felt evaporates as I see the look on his face.

"One of you stay with her. I might be letting her do this, but she's still not doing it alone."

Before I can prepare myself to follow after her, Michael's hand comes across my chest, keeping me in place.

"You are too close to the situation brother. I do believe this is where I am needed. Let me be the one to guard your beloved, the same way you have done for mine."

"I thought you hated to be hidden?" I quip and despite the way he reacted in times past, he smiles before turning toward the way Serenity has just vacated.

"That hasn't changed, but you need to stay here and prepare Graham for what happens next. It is only a matter of time before Lucifer makes his next move and we need to be as prepared as possible for whatever that may be."

I cannot argue with him. As much as I want to be the one to watch over Serenity, I know I cannot be. I am too close. My place really is here with Graham.

"Take care of her, Michael. Do not let Lucifer do what he has done in times past. This time has to be the end."

It's only when Michael disappears that I turn to Graham and motion toward the dorm.

"What does Michael mean by you preparing me?"

"As much as I wish to keep you out of this, I do believe the time for that has passed. In order to bring Serenity back we are going to have to do something I never thought would happen again."

"What's that?"

"We're going to join. The power of two is infinitely better than what we would be separately."

"You wanna ride around in my skin again? What does that solve?"

"It will be the very thing that brings about the end we both want."

"Lucifer dead?"

"Serenity safe."

He surprises me with his next words. Where I always knew him to be strong and able, he had every right not to want to join with me after the disastrous way it turned out the last time we were in this position.

"Well, what are you waiting for?"

Lucifer

It is hard not to see what Ryan did when he came into contact with her months ago as I stand here watching her. If I had known at the time that they would connect the way they did, I might have stepped in and put an end to it earlier, but there can be no denial of the reason it happened at all.

She is bathed in the purest light. It radiates off of her so brightly I am surprised she hasn't noticed it before now. She is breathtaking and if I can notice it with as much darkness residing inside of me, it is only natural that Ryan did as well. It had been my first mistake.

When one wants a job done, they must always rely on themselves before any other, though I cannot say with certainty that she would not have gotten to me in the same way that she did him. Her light, the way she carries herself makes that an undeniable truth.

The minute I came upon her, I made the decision and now I am determined to see it through. I have no doubt that my brothers have informed her of the truth. She is now aware that Ryan is merely a means to an end. I can only hope that in telling her the truth, along with preparing her for the inevitable, she will come easily and not turn this situation into something even more tragic.

If that does happen though, the life of her very soul mate is on the line. It also helps that in walking around in this body the way I am, I also have Ryan that I can use against her. She may know the truth, but that does not mean she knows the extent of it. Possessing someone, I could be doing it because he is weak, not dead. Those are the avenues I will use should this not go the way I need it to.

"Serenity."

"Who's talking this time? Lucifer or Ryan?"

"I see they wasted no time informing you of my deception."

"Why do it at all? If you want to finish what you started in Green Haven, why not just come to me as yourself?"

"I thought that in doing it this way, you would be more apt to join with me. I was wrong."

She turns and the level of shock on her face surprises me. Surely me admitting to my own failings cannot be that much of a surprise? Had Ryan not explained me at all during their time together?

"Did you just admit you did something wrong?"

"It would appear as though I did."

"So, you followed me. What exactly do you want?"

"I do believe you know what I want."

"Using me to end the world."

The matter of fact way she says it, already knowing and coming to terms with it pleases me. Where I would have expected her to attempt to flee, or back away in fright now that I am here, she is not. This may go easier than I imagine.

"It is no secret that in order for me to complete what I started in Green Haven, I need your blood. We must also change our current location. You misunderstand the rest and I do believe it is time I shed some light on what it is I am trying to accomplish."

"What does it even matter? You want to end existence for the humans, killing me in the process all because you and your daddy don't see eye."

"There is far more to it than that, Serenity. It is not as cut and dry as you believe it to be."

"So explain. I don't wanna hear it, I don't even care why you're doing it, but go ahead. Tell me your truth, Lucifer."

Something is not right about this. She is far too accepting. I want her to be of course, but her lack of caring, it is real. She speaks the truth, she has nothing left. She will not fight me and for some reason, I cannot go forward if she is this complacent.

"Serenity."

"What?"

"Explain to me why you are filled with such emptiness?"

"Isn't that the way you want me to be?"

"No."

"I can't even believe this is happening right now. I'm standing here in the middle of a freaking park talking to you like we're friends or something. Like you don't want to grab me, rip my wrists open and watch all my blood drain out."

"Right now, ripping you apart is the last thing I want to do."

"Did you suddenly grow a heart?"

I am aware of what this is about now. Knowing that Ryan is dead and it is just me filling his form, has put her right back into the dark state of mind she was in when he perished over a month ago. All of the work Graham Hudson did, it has broken down and she is becoming a shell of her former self again.

"Despite what you believe about me, I have always had a heart. It is just recently I see no point in letting it show. Serenity, the way you are reacting, I am sorry. Choosing Ryan as a means to get to you, seemed right at the time but I am seeing now that is not what I wanted at all."

"Let me guess. You wanted more of a fight?"

"Something like that, yes."

"If I don't agree to go with you; have you take me back to Green Haven and finish what you started, what happens?"

"I do believe you know what I will do."

"You're gonna go after Graham and Emma, aren't you?"

The truth is, I did not give the roommate a second thought. If my plan went off without a hitch then she would be destroyed with the rest of the world. Graham was the one I knew would cause the most damage and bend her to my will. I do not wish to tell her all of this, revealing my plan, but for some reason I am unable to ascertain, I am going to do it.

"Graham yes, Emma no."

"Of course. It doesn't matter that they mean the same thing to me, you only see the bond as something you can destroy and twist."

"Is there any sense in denying it?"

"No Lucifer, there isn't. You're more transparent then you believe yourself to be. I'm damned if I do and damned if I don't because in the end Graham will still be hurt; won't he?"

I merely nod and she lets the tears that I saw forming earlier fall from her eyes. It is the one instance of real emotion I have seen in the time we've been together and I am not quite sure what to do with it. She is not supposed to get to me this way, so why in the world is she? With all the power I hold inside me, she should not be able to break through my walls yet is doing so flawlessly.

"You said you wanted to explain things to me."

"I did."

"Now's your chance. Make me understand why you're doing this and then, I do believe we have somewhere we need to be."

She is freely giving herself to me. I should be over the moon with this knowledge but it awakens something inside of me I thought long dead. She is reminding me of myself, both the past and present versions and it is a reminder I do not wish to have.

"I know the way it will appear, but I believe my father needs to pay for all that he has done. The only way I can see him getting what I believe he deserves is not only to destroy the very creation he thinks so highly of, but also the ball of light that he put everything he has into."

"Not answering my question." She states as she begins walking toward me. It's only when she stands directly before me, her hand reaching out until it comes into contact with my own, or rather Ryan's that I witness just how powerful she truly is.

She is wrapping herself up around the darkest parts of me and attempting to soften them. She had no idea she's even doing it. Serenity is so much more than what I believed her to be at the start. It's the way she reaches out to me now that what I want changes.

I no longer want to drain her. I want her to rule with me.

"Would it help if I said I am nothing more than a child that has had his father's love taken away, so I am retaliating?"

"Not really. I already knew that."

The way she smiles as she says it, makes everything I have just realized even more important. I knew she was special when I chose her. I just had no idea at the time that she come to mean quite this much.

"If you are aware of that then there is nothing I can say that you are not already aware of. We are not so different, you and me."

"I don't know if I would go that far. I am not the one standing here thinking of ways to end your life."

"That is the furthest thing from my mind at this time Serenity. I do believe we've moved past that."

"Yet you haven't given up on the plan to end the world, have you?"

"No. I do not believe that will ever happen."

"So what happens now?"

This is the part I am unsure of. When I came in with the original plan, I believed that I would use her much as I had Ryan, a means to an end. I would garner what I needed from her and end her life. With that no longer being the case, I am not sure how to proceed. The only thing I do know for certain is that whatever it is, I want her by my side.

"I do believe we need to make our way to Green Haven. It is there where everything began and so it shall be there that everything comes to an end."

Bridging the gap even more between us, she stands before me, her hair blowing in the wind, her face giving away nothing, but her eyes shining. She is more than ready for what awaits her and the pleasure that I derived from her the first time I was near her this way weeks ago, I have again, but for different reasons. This time, the choice is hers and there had been no branding on her soul needed.

This time, she is most definitely mine.

Chapter Eighteen

The End Justifies the Means

Graham

I think after the first time, joining with Gabriel has become easier. I feel like a pro at it now because when we joined this time, I barely even felt it. Sure, the nausea was there just like it was the first time, but I didn't feel the weightlessness, the overpowering fullness that occurred the first time around and I'm freaking thankful.

The thing is, I'm messed up enough already and the last thing I wanna do is add anything physical to it. It's been hours since Serenity said she wanted to go off alone and there hasn't been a text, a call or even a smoke signal to let me know that wherever she is, she's alright.

I want her to be alright but I get why she's not. Even though it's not Ryan walking around the way we originally thought, it's still his presence that's here and it's the sight of him that pushed her to the lengths she went, the ones I had to bring her back from. It's only natural even knowing Lucifer is controlling it that the switch I turned back on inside of her days ago would be pushed back down into the off position.

If it were happening to me, I would be the same way.

I hate that she's pulling inside of herself again. That instead of staying and hashing this out with me, she had to run. I told her before that I wanted to be her safe place to fall and I thought with the way she was responding she understood that and accepted it, but her instant need to bolt is proving otherwise. I didn't wanna make light of the way she felt about Ryan, but shit, I hoped that I would be able to get past him and own her heart the way she so completely owns mine.

"I know I need to calm down, but man, is this normal? Shouldn't we have heard something from Michael by now?"

If breaking away from her will cause him to miss something of vital importance, he will not do it. Not hearing from him right now makes sense.

"So we're just supposed to sit around and wait for one of them to come through that door?"

Michael will not use the door, Graham. He enjoys sneaking up on those that are unsuspecting, but yes, in a sense that is exactly what we must do.

There's no better time than now for me to get answers about why we had to join this way at all. I know he told me some stuff outside, but I get the feeling there's more to it and I want to make sure before I head into whatever comes next that I have as much information as possible. I might have been a weak link before but I'm determined not to be this time around.

"So I know what you said about us joining, but you wanna tell me why we had to do it so early? I mean if we aren't hearing from either of them for a while, isn't it better that we're apart?"

We are joined now because I know the way my Lucifer operates. He wishes to own Serenity, whether that be through her blood or her physical form and in order to gain access to that he will reach out to the person that she cares for most. With Ryan gone, that falls to you.

Well that makes sense. The way we feel about each other means that I'm a target. I've been a target from the beginning but after what Gabriel explained to me, the lack of knowledge that Lucifer seemed to have about us being soul mates, it explains why he never came after me directly before. Now though, all bets were off. I'm a sitting duck.

Now you see why it was of utmost importance that we join. I will not let anything happen to you, Graham. If he does show up here the way I imagine, we will be ready.

"Would he kill me in order to get Serenity to do what he wants?"

With Lucifer anything is possible.

Before I can ask him more, the room lights up, but unlike before, Michael's arrival makes the lights above me shake and burst with the power of his own.

"There is no statement truer in this moment then the one you just spoken, Gabriel. I have much that I need to discuss with you."

"Why do I get the feeling that this isn't gonna be good news?" I ask and Michael turns toward me, his face pained for the first time since we met. The angels may like to beat around the bush and speak in ways that are often times hard to understand, but there can be no mistaking that look now. It says more than his words ever could.

"She has gone willingly with Lucifer. They are travelling back to the place where it all began."

"She did what?"

No. See, Serenity wouldn't do this. She knows that he's playing a game with her, that nothing he says can be trusted and in the end he will use her and destroy her just the way he wanted to do weeks ago. Going with him would be like giving up on her life and ending it herself. She's not in that place now, she's better. He can't be right.

"I'm sorry Graham, but there can be no mistaking what I heard. Though it does appear as though Lucifer has taken a different avenue then the one I expected."

What does that mean Michael?

"Lucifer is the king of deception when he needs to be, but what I witnessed between the two of them, there was no deception involved. He has told her everything that he wishes to accomplish and she made the choice willingly to go with him."

"What did he tell her?"

"She asked what would happen if she fought against what he wanted and he told her the truth. What he would do to the vessel and also what he would do to you, Graham. Appearing as Ryan, I do believe it set back everything to the way it was

171 | P a g e

before you arrived and now with all hope on her end lost, she is doing the only thing left that she can."

"Which is?"

"Protecting you."

This doesn't sit right with me. I've got one of the most powerful angels in existence riding around in my skin right now, even if he is letting me have the control. There is no way she needs to do anything to protect me. Gabriel has it covered.

"Serenity is not aware of the steps the two of you have taken, so I do believe that in order for her to go through with what happens next, she has to feel secure in the knowledge that the keeper of her heart is safe."

Keeper of her heart.

Well, that's a new one.

"Do you wish to stand here and argue with me about what I have just called you?" Michael snaps and I just shake my head.

"No, of course not. I've just never heard it before."

"You are her soul mate Graham. Of all the beings in the world your soul is the one she calls to. It makes perfect sense that she would do all of this now. The issue at present is how are we going to stop it?"

Before I can answer or even ask the questions that are floating around in my head, Gabriel speaks for me.

What exactly are we stopping, Michael? What had she agreed to?

"She believes that he wants to take her life from her, but that is not his intent at all. I am shocked that I am even able to do it, but I picked up on his thoughts during my time watching them. It appears as though he wishes to go through with the original plan."

He wishes to make her his bride.

The way Gabriel says it, as if its common knowledge turns me inside out. I knew about this, but the plan changed so quickly after I learned of it that I figured there was no way Lucifer would want to go back. It seems I was wrong.

There is still hope. If she did not agree to be his bride, to rule with him then there is still a way we can get her out of this and save the world before Lucifer brings it to its knees.

"If we're going to do this, we need to do it now, but I do believe there is somewhere we need to go first."

"Where?" I ask, finally throwing myself back into the conversation. With Gabriel joined to me, there is no way he would want to break apart in order to go with Michael somewhere, there is too much risk involved. It means that whatever steps we take next, I'm coming along for the ride.

"We need to go home. I do believe the only way we can stand before Lucifer again is with Father's help."

"How exactly is he going to help?"

"He's going to give us what we need in order to finish our fallen brother once and for all. It is time that he tells us all that he knows about the old power."

"So, Gabe's gonna need to take control again?"

"Yes, Graham. For the duration of our time at home, you will be a backseat participant. Can you handle that?"

"If it means saving Serenity, then I can handle anything. Let's do this."

Gabriel

I always knew that when everything was said and done, I would find myself here again. Armed with the knowledge that Michael provided me, there is only one option left in the war against Lucifer now that he had a most willing Serenity on his side.

My father.

Not only does he command the very power Lucifer has somehow gotten a hold of, but he also knows how to defeat it. With Ryan's passing, a pure angel will not be the thing that defeats him now, but I have no doubt that there are still other options that for whatever reason Father has not felt the need to share with us.

It is those that we need now and it appears as though Michael agrees.

'There is no need to explain why you are here. I have seen all that has taken place. I am also aware of what you need from me. I do believe it is time I arm you with the weapon you will need to end Lucifer once and for all."

Father never speaks about things unless there is no other alternative. In a sense he is the ultimate secret keeper because in knowing all the way he does, he is always prepared for what will happen next and he holds onto it tightly until there comes a time where he has to loosen his grip.

This is one of those times and I am thankful that we do not have to sit here and rehash all that has taken place in order to get him to see our side of things. He has been made aware and it is now time to move forward accordingly. He will help us end Lucifer's reign and in the process save countless lives as well as bring Serenity back where she belongs.

Even though I know in doing so it will mean far more than her just saving the world.

"Michael and Gabriel, you must head to the church in Green Haven. Lucifer as I am sure you know will be expecting you. What he will not be expecting is what is to happen once you have arrived."

"What have you planned in our absence?"

"It is true that Lucifer is in control of the same power that I have at my disposal and it is that power that is the only thing that can bring him to his knees now. What I need from the both of you is to keep him occupied long enough for me to focus that energy onto the one piece of the puzzle he has not given much thought to."

"Which is?" Michael asks, genuinely curious about what Father could mean since there has been no secret weapon up until this point at our disposal. If there had been, Michael of all beings would have been the one to find it.

"His vessel."

"You wish to somehow use Ryan in bringing about his end?"

"Ryan and Serenity both, yes."

"How?"

"Gabriel, as much as I would like to reveal everything to you, there is still the matter of the connection between you and Lucifer. I fear exposing the entire plan could spell disaster. I am sorry for how that sounds, I do have faith in you and your ability, but one cannot dispute what he did to you the last time. I do not wish to repeat the same mistake again."

He is not intending to wound me, but I cannot help that he does. It is no secret Lucifer stepped inside my mind not all that long ago and manipulated me in a way that could have cost us everything. He had not won of course, but Father did have a point. Because of the way Lucifer and I have always been with one another, I am a risk even though I do not want to be.

"Well, what do you want us to do?"

"Distract him. Michael will take the lead on that. I want you to break away at the first opportunity and make your way to Serenity. I am aware that you are joined with the soul mate and I wish you to remain that way. Use his bond with her, have him connect with her in the way that he has in times past and bring her back to us. Then, the rest of the plan will reveal itself."

"That's it? That is all you are willing to tell us? We must do all of this and then everything will be revealed? Father, what if things do not go according to plan?" Michael's voice booms around me, his tone angry; the first time since the incident with his beloved that I have ever seen him this livid with our creator.

"You must not doubt what we are about to do, Michael. I know you do not like my answer, I can feel the distrust rolling off of you in waves as we speak, but things will work out. I have seen how this plays out in the end."

"Father, I do not mean to question you in this way," he states, his voice now even, his place again realized. "But surely you have seen the free will that resides so deeply inside your ball of light. You may have seen the way this all plays out but one move on her part could change the course of that plan forever."

"I am aware of that, in fact, I am expecting it to do just that."

"What does that mean?"

"All will be revealed when the time is right. Both of you need to be on your way to Green Haven. As you make your descent, I want to you remember one thing."

"What is that?" I ask as Michael has now turned from him and is readying himself for departure.

"Have faith in me. What I have seen will come to pass. Do not let the seed of doubt override what must happen now. Everything will be as it is meant to be."

Accepting all that he has said, I do as my brother has done before me and ready myself for the trip that will take me to Green Haven once more. My mind is riddled with thoughts that I am unable to push away as I stand before Michael as we make our descent.

If everything is to be the way it was written and meant to be, when all is said and done would Serenity be standing by my side at the end of it? Or was Father willing to sacrifice her in order to reach a better tomorrow?

Chapter Nineteen

Pure Divinity

Serenity

It's strange the way things happen.

Having taken Ryan as a vessel, I didn't believe it would be possible for him to travel with me any other way than driving or walking, but the minute he held his hand out to me and pulled me into him, the familiar feel of Ryan surrounding me the instant we made contact, I saw a shadow spread out behind him and it only took a few seconds for me to understand what it was.

Where Gabriel and Michael have pure white feathered wings, Lucifer does not. His are grey in color and they are tinged in black, another reminder of Ryan that despite knowing he's gone, I still can't let go of. The tinge to the fallen angel's wings reminds me of the dark rim that surrounded Ryan's clouded blue eyes and it makes my heart ache for him even more.

It is only when we are completely joined together, about to take flight that I feel Lucifer's breath hot against me.

"The ache that you feel for the boy I considered a son, it is the same ache that filled him right before he made the decision to sacrifice himself in order to save you. He loved you Serenity. If you take nothing else from our time together, please take that."

This is not the way I imagined time with Lucifer to be though I can't exactly say I pictured spending much time with him at all before now. There is something different about him that I can't put my finger on. He's being honest with me, I can sense no deception and despite wanting to be pulled in any direction but his, I'm drawn to him and can't turn away.

"Why are you being this way?"

"That is a question young angel that I cannot answer. I have no explanation for this turn of events." He stops, pondering his next words and I just let myself stare. He's given me another truthful answer because where he can't explain it, I can't either. "Are you ready?"

"Yes."

Before I can enjoy the way it feels to move through time and space with him, we are landing in front of the church and where I expect him to usher me inside, hiding me away from the outside world, he doesn't. He releases his hold on me, taking a few steps toward the door of the abandoned church, but does nothing to move me along.

His allowance to let me find my own way, I use it to my advantage and I take steps toward the boarded up windows in front of me. Tracing my hands along the various colors of spray paint lining the outside, I think back to where it all came from. Standing here now, it's not Ryan I think about or even what's going to happen the minute I follow Lucifer through the doors.

I think about Graham.

The tagging on the outside of the building, he did this before I knew him. Every line drawn, word spelled out, picture created, they were done by his hand and now, reaching out and feeling it underneath my fingers, somehow makes me feel closer to him. Being here now, the reason I am agreeing so readily to all that awaits me beyond the church doors, it's for him.

I only wish he were here so that I could tell him what I'm doing and why. So I could say goodbye and make sure he knew this time just how much I love him.

"Why is this the place where it all began?" I call across to Lucifer and as his head rises, taking me in, he moves toward me, lessening the gap between us until he finds himself standing at my side.

"This is the place I landed when I fell from grace. It was not Green Haven then. It went by a far different name, but it was the place where this, the person you see now began."

"You want it to end where it started?"

It's not a question I expect him to answer, but true to his way of being lately, he does and again he does truthfully.

"In a manner of speaking yes. For me, this is not an ending, just another beginning."

"You're not wrong."

"I am unsure what you mean."

"You said we were alike before and at first, I didn't want to admit there was anything about me that was similar to you, but there is."

"How so?"

"This was a beginning for me too. When I moved here, it was my chance to start over. Not be the girl who heard voices, but really be me."

He takes in my words and merely nods his head, but where there had been the smallest bit of space between us before, he has again moved closer until our arms are touching. Where it should have been uncomfortable, it isn't. It's as if they belong there. As hard as it is to admit, I'm actually comfortable in Lucifer's presence.

"There is something that I wish to tell you Serenity and it is my hope that when I do, you do not turn away from me, from what we are experiencing together. I wish to maintain that level of comfort you feel with me."

What he has to tell me, it is causing him pain. It's hard, seeing these expressions on the face of the man I married and pledged to love for the rest of eternity. I want to turn away from it so bad, but I won't because in a way, whatever he has to say, I know I need to hear.

"I know that you believe that when we enter the church, I will be taking your life away, but that is not the case. Not any longer."

"What does that mean exactly?"

"I do not want to drain you or take the light that makes you pure away from you. I know that you may not believe that given our history, but it is the truth. I want you to continue to be everything that you are."

"Then what do you want?"

"I want you to," he breaks off, again the pained expression taking hold and causing my own heart to twist in knots at the sight. "I wish for you to be my queen. I want you to come home with me; rule with me."

Hell.

He wants me to go to Hell with him.

"Yes, though I was never fond of the name the humans gave my home. It is what I want to happen now, Serenity. Our similarities, they are too strong to deny. I am starting to believe that your place was always by my side, something I lost sight of when I realized the power inside you."

"What about your plan to end the world?"

"I still want that. I will make it come to pass. I just want you to be by my side when it happens."

I'm not stupid. I know what he's asking and how messed up it is. I also know that I don't want to be a part of any plan that destroys the world and the people that I love that will still be here when I'm gone. The problem I face now is that what he wants, for some reason I can't explain I want to be able to give to him.

He's right. We are alike. He may be evil and he may have spent his eternity twisting the lives of others for his own sick gain, but underneath all of that, his anger over what happened in Heaven, is the angel that he used to be and it's never been more obvious than it is right now.

We are all a little twisted inside. The darkness can take us over at any point. The difference between him and the rest of us is, it's what we choose to do in the moment we realize it that matters. For a lot of us that means standing and fighting back until all we're bathed in is light. For Lucifer, it's accepting the darkness because it's easier.

I'm starting to see now just what it was that made Ryan so loyal to him during their time together. If he was at all like this with him, then it makes perfect sense why they stayed together as long as they did and why going against Lucifer had been so hard on him.

The man that now has Ryan's face is giving me something back that I never thought I would ever have again. He's giving me back the boy I lost.

"I should be angry that you are comparing us, but it is true. Ryan stayed with me so long, walked through the darkness with me the way he did because we were very similar. Two lost beings that made choices others could not understand, ones that set us apart from the rest of the world around us. His human in nature and mine celestial. In every way that he could be, he was my son and I wish nothing more than to give him back to you now."

"It's not possible though, is it?"

"In the physical way, no. I wish I could tell you otherwise but I cannot."

"He's here with us now."

I'm not sure why I say this, admit it, but I can't deny it's true. The Lucifer that came to me hours ago and the one here with me now, the truthful one despite knowing what it means, that's not the darkness talking, it's Ryan and it's because of him, the way I can feel him around me so powerfully that I'm going to do the unthinkable.

I am going to become Lucifer's queen.

Graham

The angels have a plan and it's one that for whatever reason, they believe won't go wrong and even though they've explained it all to me and I get it, I still can't see where their faith in it can be so strong.

I believe in God, despite the fact that he hasn't done a damn thing to answer my mom's prayers and she's still lying in her bed, a short distance from here fighting for her life. I want to hate the guy for not doing something for her, but I know that there's probably more at play here then I know about, so I don't.

His plan though, leaving parts out and telling his own sons that all will reveal itself in time, I think that's gonna come back to bite him in the ass. Nothing ever goes according to plan. It's the way life as a whole is designed. It's the changes, the bumps in the road, the things that happen that you don't see coming that make life worth living.

If this goes wrong though, there won't be that much living to be had because the world and all it contains will cease to exist. So for the first time ever, I'm hoping that what is written is what happens because the alternative is just too dark to imagine.

"Are you clear on what you must do now, Graham?" Michael asks, bringing me away from my thoughts.

Find Serenity.

"Yeah. We're gonna go in, you're gonna engage Lucifer and I'm going to try and talk some sense into my stubborn soul-mate. We've been over this a million times already."

You must excuse Michael, he has about as much faith in this working as you do.

"Is that true?"

"I am action oriented, Graham. I do not work well with the *all will be revealed in time* nonsense. So yes, it is true, at least in part. I do not doubt Father, but something does not feel right about this for me so I am cautious.

The word is paranoid, brother.

"Gabriel, unless you want to break away from the boy and stand beside me to fight our fallen brother, I suggest you keep your comments to yourself."

As you wish.

"Find her, Graham. The bond she is forging with Lucifer, it has gone on long enough. Remind her of what the two of you can share together if she remains with you and bring her home to us."

Having this fall back on me, it scares the shit out of me. I always thought that because I was human, there wasn't a whole hell of a lot I could offer in battle, especially going up against the devil himself, but I'm finding out now that my part is the one that will determine everything and I can't make light of it or try and push my way past it.

Lucifer will fall only if I succeed.

She is separated from him now. I can feel her light. We must make our move.

It's do or die time. This is where I step up to the plate and prove my worth, not only to the angels, but also to myself. If there's one thing I know I can do, it's this. I can bring that beautiful ball of light back to me. I've done it before and I know I can do it again because without her, there can be no Heaven.

Taking the route I've taken so many times before, I slip myself through the unlatched window at the side of the building, plunging myself into the basement and wasting no time, I head for the stairs, taking them two at a time until I can feel exactly what the angel did seconds before and I know I've hit my destination.

You can sense her light as well.

"Yeah. Not sure how, but it's pretty damn powerful."

You know what you must do now.

"I know Gabriel. I've got to bring her back to you."

That is not what I was going to say.

"If I'm not doing that, then what am I doing?"

You are to do what you were born to do. This; Graham Hudson, is your destiny.

Placing my hand on the knob and turning it, Gabriel's words, the truth, rolling around in my head, pushing me forward, I slide the door open and take the slow steps inside. It's only when the door clicks shut behind me, having kicked it with my boot that the vision before me now turns around and the angel's words are driven home again.

Serenity, saving her, bringing her back into the light, it really is what I was born to do and now it's time to do it and this time make it stick.

Serenity

Making my choice, choosing to do things this way, it was supposed to keep him safe, but it's not doing that at all because not only is he not far away from here the way I need him to be, but he's not alone.

I can tell by the light around him that Gabriel is with him, which means Michael can't be far behind. I should have seen this coming. I thought in breaking away from the three of them, going off on my own that this would go off the way I needed it too. If the world had to end, if Graham and the angels had to be lost to me, it would happen far away from here.

I wouldn't have to deal with the fallout of my selfish actions.

"Graham, you shouldn't be here. If he finds out there's no telling what he'll do."

"I don't care."

"You need to care."

"The only thing that matters to me is you, Serenity. Lucifer can do whatever the hell he wants to me and as long as I know that you're okay, I'll take it all."

"Don't say things like that. You deserve better than this."

"And you don't? Are you really that far gone? Has he gotten to you that much already?"

He moves toward me and I back away. I know what will happen the minute we touch and it just can't. The bond we share, the connection we have, now is not the time for it to ignite. If it does it will ruin everything.

"Stop trying to sacrifice yourself to save me, Serenity. If it's my time to go, then I'm ready to go. It's my choice, not yours."

He's right of course, but the same could be said for me. It's my choice to want to do things this way. To give myself completely to Lucifer in an effort to change the way he has it all planned out. I've seen the effect I have on the fallen angel. I know if I do this, I can stop him from destroying the world. I know I have it in me, but not if he doesn't let me go through with this now.

"You need to go."

"I'm not going anywhere."

"Graham..."

"No, Serenity. I already know what you're going to say. You're gonna sit here and tell me that you need to do this; that it's the only way you can guarantee I'm gonna be safe. That we'll make it out of here alive, but you're wrong and I don't want to hear it."

"Then what do you wanna hear?"

"Why you think you need to do this."

"You haven't seen the things I've seen, Graham. Do you know I can still smell the scent of my blood when Ryan was draining it that day? That I'm haunted by the pain I saw in his eyes knowing he was taking my life away from me?"

"I don't need to see them to know what you went through! Don't you get it? I feel it every single time we're together. Every time we touch, we connect and everything you're feeling, the horrors you've been through, I feel like I've lived through them too! You might think you need to give up here, that doing this is the only way out, but it's not. You need to stop this and you need to fight with me instead of for me."

"Lucifer; he's not the same as he was before, Graham. I can get through to him. If you just let me do this, I can stop what he's got planned. He cares for me, I know I can change things, but I can't if you stay."

"Stop talking and listen!" he yells at me and I flinch. This is not a side of Graham that I've ever seen before. I know Gabriel is attached to him and I want nothing more than to blame the angel for this change now, but I can't because Gabriel has never been this way with me either.

"I am not leaving here and you are not doing this. You are not going to give yourself to Lucifer in hopes that you can change his mind because for some reason he's made you believe he's somehow better than he is. He is the devil Ser! He will make you believe the sky is falling if it gets him what he wants! You need to see that and stop this right now. I can't lose you!"

"If I don't go through with this, he's going to kill you, Graham. You and the entire world and I don't even wanna think about what he's going to do with Heaven."

"You're doing this for Gabriel too?"

"Yes. I'm doing it for all of you. You said you can't lose me, well I can't lose you either. I don't care what happens to me, but I can't let anything happen to you."

"If you do this, you're going to kill me, Ser. We've been separated in every lifetime we've ever been in together and right now, you're gonna do something that willingly brings it around again."

He's right. I don't want to admit it, but for once, I can't argue this. We have been torn from each other in every lifetime we've lived before and I made him a promise that it wouldn't happen this time around. We would never be taken from each other again, yet with what I'm about to do, I'm breaking it.

I'm allowing us to be taken from each other before we've had the chance to experience what it feels like to be together. If I thought my decision was selfish before, it's even worse now.

"Don't do this. You can end this now. God; he's got a way out of this, but you need to come with me now. We need to finish this."

"What are you talking about? God has a way out of this, how?"

"Come with me and find out."

If I walk from this room right now, I am putting Graham at risk. The boy that noticed me sitting by a tree when we were sixteen years old and went out of his way to make himself a part of my life, this boy that showed me what love really is, I risk putting him and all that he is in danger.

Weighing that against the knowledge that in doing so I'm keeping my promise to that same boy that I care for so deeply, it's threatening to tear me apart. I don't want to lose him in another lifetime, I don't want to lose him at all.

"Serenity, I love you. We're going to get through this and both of us are gonna be okay, but not if you do what you think you have to do. You already lost Ryan and it almost destroyed you, please don't do the same thing to me. Don't make me lose you, not when I just found you again."

The room falls silent as I think over everything I know to be true and all of things that I want to be true based on my actions here before he showed up. I need to make a choice and I have to do it now. This moment, it's what God put in motion when he created me.

This is my destiny.

"Ser, talk to me. Don't shut me out."

"I know what I've gotta do now."

"What's that?"

"The right thing. For everyone."

Lucifer

There have been many times where I pictured what it would be like to stand before Michael again, but in every vision I had of the event, it was never quite like this.

His body is frozen in place, sword at the ready, waiting for me to take one small step toward him so that he can recreate the very events that changed the way we both have existed so very long ago. He wishes to do now the very same thing as he did then, only this time, bring about my true death in the process.

He does not realize that I am aware, but when he cast me from Heaven, it damaged him. In all the battles I have witnessed him be a part of, there has been one common theme. He has always been cold, calculated and unfeeling. Banishing me from Heaven brought that about in him. It was never supposed to be his path, but it is one that he has come to terms with and accepted easily.

"I do not wish to fight you, Michael; you can put the blade away."

"You forget who you are speaking with. I know you better than you know yourself. All of this is happening for a reason and I will not allow it. The weapon stays."

"What do you believe I am here to accomplish?"

"You wish to destroy Heaven by corrupting its greatest gift and from there you wish to destroy the world. It has been your end game for quite some time and as I have said, I will not allow it."

"Michael, I know you were there when I spoke with Serenity. You know my true motivation now."

"You still wish to end the world."

"Maybe so, but not before making Serenity mine."

"Why do you want her so badly? In the beginning I understood why, the blood that pumps so strongly in her veins, it is enticing to you. The power behind it, it draws you in and owning it so completely would give you control. What I do not seem to get is the change I sense in you as it pertains to her."

"I could explain it to you, but I do not believe you would understand nor accept it as truth."

"You would be right about that, but indulge me Lucifer. You are aware of who she is, are you not? She belongs to Gabriel."

"I am well aware of who and what she is brother. I am also aware that Gabriel and she are bonded together by a force quite stronger than myself. It matters little to me."

"Do you fancy yourself in love with her? Is this what all of this is about?"

"No. I know nothing of love. What I do know is that the ball of light Father so eloquently created, she has brought something to life inside me, something I long believed dead and in order for me to foster that, I do believe I need her by my side."

"Even though you used her love for your protégé against her?"

"Yes."

It is what happens next that is most startling to me. Where Michael had been sure to keep his weapon at the ready, he is now standing down and where it had been front and center before, it falls to the background. He now understands that I am not here to go to war with him. I am merely here to finish what I should have months before.

Making Serenity mine.

"Gabriel will not allow you to have her. Despite the bond the two of you share, having spent as much time together as you did back home, he will go to his death before giving her over to you."

"Of that I am aware."

"Does it not bother you at all, what owning her will do to him?"

"It does, but it is how it must be."

There is a noise from the right hand side of the room and as I turn toward it, I see not only Serenity making her way toward me, but Graham following closely on her heels. It is only when I see the light make its way into the room that I realize what is going on.

Graham is not alone. Gabriel is with him.

"Michael is right." Graham says, though his voice has taken on a completely different tone then I am used to, proving that it is indeed Gabriel guiding him now.

"Our brother has said quite a lot of things before you made your entrance, Gabriel. Care to tell me which one of them is right?"

"I will not let you have Serenity, not without a fight. She is not meant for the darkness of your world Lucifer and deep inside I believe you know that."

"Maybe it is not about making her embrace my darkness. Maybe it is about me embracing her light. Did you not think of that, Gabriel?"

His head lowers and I am content in the knowledge that he now sees what lies behind everything that is taking place now. I still have every intention of doing away with both the planet and the place I used to call home, but as I told Michael, it will not happen now. All I want in the moment is to be surrounded by Serenity and her light.

"How many times did I extend the olive branch to you during our time together, Lucifer? How many times did you turn me down?"

"There is no need to bring up ancient history. I would have assumed you would just be happy I have reached this point at all."

"I am not happy about any of this. It is not meant to happen this way. If you want access to the light, then you will do so in the right way. You will not take and corrupt Serenity in order to do it."

"I do believe the choice is hers what happens now, Gabriel. I am not making her do anything. She has freely given herself to me and believes in what it is that I want. Instead of taking your anger out on me, I do believe you need to look to your beloved."

Watching as Gabriel does as I have suggested and turns toward Serenity, I feel the room begin to shift. An uneasy feeling rises in my chest and makes it way up until I find it hard to breathe. Before it completely takes me under, it occurs to me what is happening now.

Father has arrived.

God

Every step taken has been leading to this very moment.

The moment in time where I will bring to life a soul that has been lost to me in an effort to make things right.

I have always known that it would lead to this point, it had just been my hope that it would have taken place in a far better manner then it has to now.

Ryan McGregor is the purest angel in existence, apart from the ball of light that is now standing before me, a look of shock on her face as she takes in all that I have put forth. Where Ryan's body had been guided by Lucifer and his dark intentions before, I have now overridden him in favor of bringing the light to the surface. There is no doubt as her eyes take me in that she realizes what is happening.

"Ryan?" she asks, crying out before running and throwing her arms around me.

I will not let her believe for a second longer that I am indeed the pure angel returned to her, but there can be no explaining the way it feels to have her on the side of the light so completely again. We may not be related in the most biological of senses, but she is my daughter; my greatest creation and I would go to the ends of the earth to see her reach her happiness.

"It is not Ryan in the manner you remember him, but he is here with us, Serenity."

"Father." Gabriel speaks from behind her, the reality now setting in for my other son as Michaels stands guard watching over the situation, his face giving away nothing to how he feels.

"Our power levels are quite evenly matched, more so than I originally thought. If we are to do this, bring about a better ending for us all, we need to do it now. Serenity, I know this is going to be difficult, but what happens next, it is in your hands."

"What exactly do you want me to do?"

"Exorcize Lucifer from Ryan, so that I may finish him once and for all. Once that has been done, you must then turn the blade on me."

Her eyes go wide and where she embraced me minutes before she is now backing up until she finds herself in Graham's waiting arms, though Gabriel is the one holding her.

"I can't do that. You want me to kill you?"

"No child; you will not kill me, but you will set Ryan's soul free once and for all."

I know what I am asking of her. I know how hard this will be. She has already had to come to terms with him dying one time before, it will not be easy being the very cause of it again, but it is what needs to happen in order for her to reach her destiny, much the same way as her soul mate before her.

"If I do this, what happens to him? Where will Ryan go?"

"He will meet his true death; the death of a pure angel and he will cease to exist. I am aware that it is not the end you wish for him but it is better than that which he has been subjected to based on Heaven's error. Set him free Serenity, it is what is best for all involved."

She seems to think over everything I have said and I feel Lucifer fighting for control. It is only a matter of seconds before he will again rise to the surface. Her choice, it needs to happen now before everything we have fought for falls apart before our very eyes.

"Make the right choice Serenity—for me."

Her head rises and her eyes lock on mine and I can tell that what has been said has reached its mark. Ryan, having spent the time in Purgatory after his death, is indeed gone, but his soul, despite that is still able to reach out and now, as her eyes go wide and reality sets in, she steps forward again.

"Let him take control." She whispers, giving me all that I need and as I take the step backward again letting Lucifer rise to the surface, I watch in awe as she does what she has been born to do.

She brings about the end of the darkness, once and for all.

Serenity

"Vi esorcizzare, ogni spirito impuro. Ogni potere satanico, ogni incursion Dell'avversario infernale, ogni legione, Fand la congregazione e la setta diabolica. Così, maledetto demone, e ogni legione diabolica, noi scongiuriamo voi. Cessate ingannare le umane creature e dando loro il veleno della perdizione eterna."

I have no idea how I'm even doing this, the words falling from my lips almost as if they have a mind of their own, but once I start, I can't stop. All it took was God standing before me, giving Ryan the chance to speak, telling me to do right by him and here I am doing the right thing.

This is what I knew would happen when I told Graham it was time. Not only did I make him a promise that meant more to me than whatever Hell or Heaven had in store for me, but I also made Ryan a promise.

I would continue to live for him, fight for him even if we didn't find a way out of the church the last time we were here, and now it's my chance to do right by the both of them, loving them as completely as I do. One gone, but not forgotten and the other very much alive and waiting for me on the other side.

As the final word falls, I see Ryan's body crumple to the floor and the essence of the fallen angel before me now, his gray wings now completely black and the light that had surrounded him before completely gone, an orb of black left in its place.

This is Lucifer in his true form. The being I almost pledged to stand beside for the rest of my life.

Michael moves toward him and before I realize what is going on, I see the silver sword moving toward me, falling effortlessly into my hand and it's then that I know what has to happen next. In order for Lucifer to meet his end, I need to be sure that Ryan meets his even though his happened weeks before.

As Michael tries to keep Lucifer subdued, I move toward Ryan, reaching him and bending down, taking him in one final time, remembering him for the way he looks now and the way he looked that day in the church, and stepping back slightly, rising to my feet, I do the only thing left to do and I raise the weapon.

Gabriel, in Graham's body screams from behind me, telling me it's time and raising the sword as high in the air as I can, I close my eyes tightly, whispering my own private goodbye before bringing it down hard and fast, hearing as it pierces through his chest cavity until it slices completely through to the other side.

Backing away quickly, I turn and that's when I see what God had been trying to tell me. Lucifer's form begins to break away, piece by piece and in the time it takes me to blink a few times, coming to terms with what I'm seeing, the final piece breaks apart, leaving nothing but trail of dust in its wake.

He's gone.

All of this, it's too much to take. Before I realize what's happening, my knees hit the floor and I can feel the water pouring from my eyes. Tears, though I'm so numb now, I can't control them as they fall. I'm not crying for Lucifer, though my heart seems to hurt for what his final fate is. The tears, they're for Ryan because no matter where I go from here or what happens now, the reality will never change.

He's gone too.

Forever.

Chapter Twenty

Two Become One

Serenity

I can't believe everything I've been through has led me to this point. Standing before God, Graham by my side, listening as he explains to the both of us what has to happen now.

From the time I was created, my soul split in two, it's been foretold that I would end up standing exactly where I am now. The only difference is that he's here with me, way before I want him to be and he's preparing to go through with the one thing that will both join us and break us apart forever.

Now that Lucifer has been defeated, this time it having been proven that he is no longer in existence, the time has come for me to take my rightful position by God's side. It was in the final moment after Lucifer had been killed that things began to change. Not only did the light around me magnify, but I also gained the one thing that until then had been elusive and unknown.

The moment I achieved what God put in motion, I realized my true place and as such, became one of the purest angels in Heaven. Wings the color of newly fallen snow appeared around me, covering me in their warmth and it was in that moment, that I was called home and to the very place I find myself now.

Graham Hudson is my soul-mate. He is the part of me that was split before I was sent down during my first lifetime and he is the one being in all of creation that my heart calls for every moment we are not together. He is supposed to have a long life, just as I am, at least according to Michael during my previous time here, but it appears as though the plan has changed.

He stands with me now because with Lucifer vanquished, there is nothing more that the two of us as a unit need to accomplish. All that is left now is for the very being that created us to put us back together.

I'm not sure how I feel about that. Having reconnected with Graham again after such a long period of time without one another, I thought we would have more time to enjoy each other and all that being connected in the way we are brings. I couldn't have been more wrong. Just as I experience what it means to be with the true keeper of my heart, it is being taken from me and the tremendous loss I felt when Ryan was stripped away is back again, only magnified because of who and what Graham is to me.

Being joined back together should bring me a level of happiness of which I've never known, but all it does is make me feel sad. The moment when we are put back together again, one complete soul, I may become stronger and more powerful as a light of Heaven, but I would still be without the best parts of myself because Graham will cease to be Graham. He will be me.

Gabriel has tried explaining all of this to me. The moment he heard that his Father had called us home, he made it a point to prepare me for what was going to happen next, especially after he learned I wouldn't be making the trip alone. The thing is, there can be no right amount of preparation, just as there can be no right reaction.

I am both gaining and losing Graham and there is nothing I can do about it.

"I know that what is about to take place causes you pain Serenity, but you always knew this day would come."

"You're right. I just never thought it would be this quickly. Why bring us back together if you planned on ripping us apart again directly afterward?"

"Ser, he's not ripping us apart. If anything, I think he's putting back together what he broke all those years ago."

There he is. The man that I love so completely. Seeing things in a way that I'm not able to because I can only think in terms of loss. I may be an angel now, but underneath it all, I am still me and nothing that takes the very real man standing beside me away will ever be seen as right.

I'm not sure I can handle another loss, even though to everyone surrounding me it isn't a loss at all.

"You have done the world and Heaven a great service, Serenity. That is what you must focus on as we progress forward. What Graham has said to you is true. I am merely putting together that which I split apart centuries ago. I am making you whole again."

"I don't mean any disrespect, but if you knew anything about me, the human me, you would know that I was already whole. Graham made me that way. Putting us back together may be making me whole in the biblical sense, but it will not in the emotional one."

The strangest thing happens after I finish speaking. He laughs and it's only after I search not only Graham's face for some kind of understanding, but Michael and Gabriel's that he finally steps forward and gives me a reason for the sudden outburst.

"You must forgive me, but until this very moment, I could not understand how you were to be Gabriel's beloved. It is in the stubbornness you display at what you know to be the truth, what must happen next that opens my eyes. You are indeed like Michael before you. Neither one of you could accept things easily."

"Father, I must disagree with you. I am nothing like the pure angel."

"That is where I beg to differ with you, my son. Let me remind you of the stubborn way you reacted when faced with a situation quite like this one. The only difference between then and now is that she is not leaving Heaven because of it."

The way Michael backs down makes me curious to know what God is talking about. I do see his point though. If anything that's why I had such a hard time in my past dealings with the elder archangel. We are too alike for our own good. He is just as set in his ways as I am, though I am willing to listen, learn and change my opinion over time where he isn't.

"I am glad that you are able to see that Serenity. You and Michael are not so different after all."

"I've always known that at some point Graham and I would be brought back together again. Gabriel explained that much to me before we faced Lucifer the first time, but Michael stood beside me and said that I would have a long life ahead of me. In order to truly understand what we're doing here now, I need to know what changed."

"When Ryan passed, what was written changed. Things did not happen the way they were meant to. That is why things are not as they have been told. In order to adapt to the rift that Ryan's death caused, we needed to change the timetable."

"So if Ryan lived that day, then this wouldn't be happening now."

"Correct."

I still don't like this, but I'm starting to get it. None of what happened back then was supposed to happen that way. Ryan was never supposed to be in the church at all based on everything we know about him now. It's only natural that with the story being changed, this had to change too.

"Okay. If this is what needs to happen then I'm ready for it, but if it's possible, can I have a few moments alone with Graham before we go through with it?"

"Of course. Take whatever time you need and be sure that everything that you need to say to one another is said because once you are joined, you will never have the chance to go back."

"Obviously." I think, realizing too late that not only did I think it, but I said it out loud as well. "Sorry."

"It is alright, Serenity. Gabriel, Michael and myself, we will take our leave of you now. When the time has come for us to move forward, we will let you know."

True to his word, all three of them disappear and it's just Graham and me. It's turning to him now, looking at him, really taking him in for what I know now is the final time that I allow the tears that have been building on the surface to fall.

I really don't want to say goodbye to him, not when it feels like I've just said hello.

With as right as everything has felt between us from the first moment we laid eyes on each other, everything in the moment now screams wrong and I want to run from it, escape altogether the way Michael apparently did before me, but the look in his eyes, the acceptance of what's to come, it stops me cold.

I can't run from this. I can't run from him.

Graham

I don't want to admit it in front of God and the others, but I hate this as much as she does. I'm not looking forward to what happens next. I may not know everything there is to know about our previous lifetimes together, but what I do know is that they always end up with us being torn apart from each other.

This, putting both of us back together so that we're one complete soul, it's supposed to be different than all the times before, but for me it's not. It's like losing her all over again and it's just not something I can accept.

Now that we're alone and she's looking at me, those hazel eyes able to see parts of me that no other person in the world can or will ever be able to see, it's almost too much to take. I have to resist the urge to look away because standing in her presence this way is too overwhelming.

"I hate this."

"I was wondering if you were going to admit it. Thanks for letting me argue it alone." She laughs and my heart sinks a little more. When they do whatever it is they're going to do, I'm never going to hear that sound again. It's never going to affect me quite the way it does now. Everything really is going to change.

"You argue so much better than me."

"You're right about that. I do. I'm thinking I would have made a pretty badass lawyer."

"I can't say goodbye to you." I whisper, reaching out as the words fall and pulling her into me, needing to experience what it feels like to have her in my arms, even if it is the final time. "We should bail on this whole thing and run away together."

"If only it were that easy."

She's right. If it was that easy I have a feeling we would have done it already. We wouldn't have stood around here and debated it the way we did, instead just disappearing before their eyes and hiding out until they gave up looking for us. It's not meant to work that way though. There is nowhere that we could hide that the power of Heaven wouldn't find us, especially since now, she's a very real part of it.

I still can't believe the woman I'm holding is an angel now. She's always been that to me, but seeing it for myself, the wings, the bright light and the way it seems to completely cover me now that she's in my arms, it almost feels like I'm dreaming. Something like this, as beautiful and as pure as this can't be real, not in the world I've been living in for the last twenty-one years.

It's very real though and it's just another thing I'm going to miss the minute we come together. In a sense, we're both going to cease to exist, or at least I am. All of this, what we experienced together, the way I felt as I fell in love with her all over again the last couple of weeks, I'm going to lose it all and I don't want to.

"You're wrong you know."

"About what?"

"I hate this as much as you do, I think my argument earlier proves that, but I do believe that when we're put back together, we're going to take everything we went through with us. It will just be both of our experiences put together in one complete story. One point of view instead of two."

"Serenity Richards, the romantic. Who knew?" I joke, which causes her to break out into the worlds brightest grin, turning me inside out the way she always has before.

"Well, when you can't find a good love story to read, the next best thing is to create one of your own. I think I like ours better."

"I like ours better too. I'm just not sure I'm ready to give up on it quite yet. Not when there's so much more I want to do."

She pulls herself out of my arms and as the loss of her sets in, I see her hand outstretched, pointing off into the distance. It's only when I take the steps over to her and really focus on where she's pointing that I see it.

Tucker's Pond.

"How is that even possible?"

"Sometimes I forget that you've never been here before. Heaven appears the way that is most pleasurable to you. It becomes what you want to see most. For me, right now I wanted to see the pond where you confessed how you felt about me, the point where we became one again and it seems you want the same thing."

"Is it real?"

"As real as it was the day we were there."

"Sit with me?"

"I thought you'd never ask."

Taking her hand in mine, I make my way over to the very spot we found ourselves in the first time we were together and just like before, the ducks are there to greet us, making their way slowly across the still water, creating a sense of peace with every movement they make.

"Tell me the things you still want to do with me. Paint me the most beautiful picture of our life together so that no matter where I go from here, I will always have it with me."

I'm not sure if it's because of all the changes that she's been through since the battle with Lucifer or if it's just an after effect of being here in Heaven, but the comment I made as a joke earlier, hearing her now, is bringing truth to it. Serenity really has become the romantic and what she's asking me for proves it.

Wanting to know what I want with her, the things I can picture so easily in my mind about our life together, calling it a beautiful picture, it's not something that she would have said before. She's different now, but just like every other time I've noticed changes in her, I realize that she's becoming my kind of different.

Sitting on the dock, pulling her body into mine as our legs swing out over the edge, I lean my body into hers, feeling the brush of her hair against my face and relishing ever second of it, attempting as I do to find the words that she's asked me for. The ones that will give her the most beautifully bright picture to hold on to.

"I see us living together in a small two bedroom apartment off campus while we're both working and going to class. You coming home from work and catching me painting and a small kiss turning into more until we're both covered in paint, but laughing. Happy. I see you walking toward me in the world's longest wedding dress, your face covered by the veil, but my eyes somehow able to see through it enough to connect to yours. I see us married and having children. You carrying my children."

"How many?"

"Two. A boy that has your eyes and hair color and a little girl that has mine. I see us working together, raising them and I see them becoming even better versions of us. They're going to change the world Ser, because they've got their mothers heart and their father's strength and determination. They're going to accomplish everything that we didn't get the chance to."

"Graham..."

"Serenity, when I woke up with you this morning, it wasn't supposed to be our last morning. It was supposed to be one morning that would lead into another one and another after that until there were so many that I lost count. I want another morning with you."

"Do you remember what I told you that day at the pond?"

"You told me a lot of things, princess."

"I said that when my time came, I wanted to go knowing that I lived my life to the fullest, each day lived like it would be my last. When I left the world, I wanted to do it with no regrets. Graham, I'm doing that. What happens next, here, I'm ready for it despite not wanting it to happen this way. I have no regrets."

"Even though we won't ever get to experience that life I just told you about?"

"But we did experience it. We're sitting here now, in our own little version of Heaven and we're living the life you just painted for me. I can feel all of it as though I lived it and that's why I can do this with no regrets because I have done everything I wanted with the one person who came into my life and showed me what it feels like to really live."

The way she says it, it really is like she lived all of the things that until now have only been in my head. It's impossible of course, because none of those things happened, but for a split second it almost feels as though it has, with as clearly as I can see it.

"It did happen Graham. We are in the one place in all of existence where nothing but beauty and love reside. I know what it feels like to be loved by you, married to you, waking up to you each and every day for the rest of our natural lives. I know what it feels like to carry your child inside me and to help you raise it. I know all of this because we've lived it."

"I don't get it."

"Yes you do. Why do you think you can see it so clearly in your mind?"

"Because I want it so bad I can practically taste it?"

I know it's a stupid response, but it's all I've got. Heaven or not, I know for a fact that we didn't live through what I can see in my head. It's just a need and a want, something that once we're joined together again I will never be able to experience the way I want to.

"We're soul-mates baby, anything is possible with us, but in this case, we have lived it. What you want so badly isn't a want, it's your minds way of remembering the way we were before."

"What are you getting at? I still don't get it."

"There was another lifetime Graham, one that Gabriel didn't tell us about. We had all of that. A life together, a family, a love so powerful nothing could come between it and break it apart. We had all of that and it's those memories that you're calling on now. What you want with me in this lifetime is what we've already had."

"We didn't lose each other?"

"No. It's another way I know that God is right about us. I hate that he's right about anything, but I can't deny it. We aren't meant to lose each other. It only appeared to be that way. What we are meant to do is find each other and love each other, be changed for the better by each other and use that to change the world."

"You did that. You were the one that changed the world."

"We did it. We've done it all. If you hadn't come back into my life after Ryan died, what happened in Green Haven, facing him down again while he wore Ryan's face, I never would have been able to make it through that. I would have given myself over to the darkness and been lost forever. You didn't let me do that. You fought for me even when I couldn't. We changed the world."

"It doesn't make this any easier. I still don't think I can say goodbye to you."

"Then don't say goodbye. We're never going to be without each other. We're always going to be in each other's lives. So if you can't say goodbye, change it up."

"How do I do that?"

"You never stop saying hello."

"How is it that the girl that just argued with God and a couple of pretty big archangels is the one telling me that this is all going to be okay?"

Reconciling the Serenity from a few minutes ago with the one I'm with now is hard. She seems to have jumped completely on board with what's about to happen and while everything she's saying makes sense, I'm still sitting on the edge, not quite there with her. There's a part of me that wants her to fight harder for this, for more time together.

I'm also bothered because I know what's going to happen the minute we're joined. We're gonna become one soul again, her being the dominant part and she's going to make her life with Gabriel. Ours isn't the only bond in play here, the beloved bond is too.

Gabriel is going to be the one to experience this angel now. Not me.

"I love you Graham Hudson. What you've given to me, brought to my life, no other being in existence will ever be able to say they did. God may bring us back together and I might even end up with Gabriel, but he will never take away what we had. What we will always have. I will love you always."

"I said I would be with you forever and I meant it. We'll do this, I'll accept this has to happen, but I'm going to love you even after it's done. I'm going to love you forever. We're never ending princess."

I feel the wetness from her eyes through my shirt and I know that I'm not alone in this. She's as affected by what we're about to do, this goodbye right now as I am. This is what I want to take with me, this knowledge that despite the bond we share, I wasn't alone in everything I felt. She was right here with me the entire time.

Placing my hands on her face, bringing it up so that I'm able to look into her eyes one final time, I place my lips to hers gently, taking in not only the softness as we connect but also her scent, the glow that surrounds us because of her, all of it. I take it in and enjoy every second of it, another picture I will take with me always.

As we break away, her lips raised in a smile, I hold onto and remember everything she's told me here today and guided by it, I lean down to her and whisper my final words to her.

"I'm ready."

Epilogue

Unbreakable

Gabriel

"Gabe, I know you were sent down here to be with her, guide her and make sure that she ended up here now, but before your father goes through with this, I need you to know something."

Graham is guided by the belief that what is about to take place is what I want. He knows what will happen once they are joined and there is nothing I can say to change it because it is the truth. The one thing he is wrong about is my feelings on the matter.

I do not want the two of them to be taken from one another. I have had selfish thoughts on this matter in the past, but I do not have them any longer. Graham for the time that he had been in her life made her happy and for that I will be eternally grateful. He is the very reason she has realized her true destiny and for that among other things, he will always hold a special place within me.

He is the reason the beloved bond will be activated. I have no doubt that if he had been any other person in her life, this end would not have been reached.

"Speak freely, Graham."

"You didn't just do right by Serenity. You did right by me too. Before you came into my life, I had no idea what my purpose was. I went through the motions day to day but never really gave much thought to a bigger picture. You showed me that picture and no matter what happens next, I need you to know that just like I won't forget her, I won't forget you either."

"Graham, you are not the only one that experienced things during our time together. You have taught me what it really means to be human and to be guided by the purest light. I am a better being for my time with you and I can assure you it will never be forgotten."

"Take care of her." He says, leveling me with a look that I completely understand. He is making sure that I do what he knows I am capable of and treasure the woman he loves in his absence. "Take care of us both."

"You have my word. I will never take either of you for granted."

"When she gets stubborn with you, pushing you to your limits and trust me she will, don't get frustrated and walk away. Stand beside her and fight. I'm pretty sure you're gonna do it anyway, but never take her, her heart and soul for granted. Make sure she never forgets that she's everything."

I admire him more in this moment then I believe I have ever done in our short time together. He does not want this to be the end, he struggles with it deep inside, but he is moving forward despite that. He is making sure that I treat her the way he always did and he has nothing to worry about.

I'm aware of the gift I am being given in Serenity and not a moment will go by in our life together where I will ever forget it or take it for granted. She will be mine and there will never be a time where she is not showered in all the love that my heart and heaven have.

"You have my solemn promise Graham."

"Then I guess that's it. Let's get this over with."

We both turn toward Father and as he moves forward, bringing himself to stand before us, he turns to Serenity first and lifts her hands into his.

"Do not fear what happens next. Please place your hands into Graham's so we may begin."

The light that is evident in this moment, my own shining through, joining with Fathers and then Serenity's covering not only herself but Graham as well, it appears as though Heaven has never been more lit up, more alive. This is not the first time

I have witnessed two souls coming back together as one, but it is the one that I most invested in.

There has never been a more beautiful sight than the one I am witnessing now.

Doing as Father has asked of her, they turn toward one another, the smiles never once leaving either of their faces, proving again just how accepted this next step is.

Father lifts his hands and watching intently, I witness his light surround both Graham and Serenity as they stand connected as one. It is then that his lips part and he speaks the words that along with the power of his light, will change everything forever.

"Ti prendo mani nelle mie, e con questo il nastro io intrecciano. Il tuo amore ti legano per sempre, da ora fino alla fine del tempo. Questo è il momento in cui due diventano uno."

The moment where two become one.

Right before my eyes, Father is binding them together and the light that had been evident in Graham's eyes begins to dim as his soul begins to lift from his body, the trail of blue travelling across the small space between the two of them and surrounding Serenity.

Her eyes close as she opens herself completely to the connection and it is in that moment, where she completely accepts the missing part of her soul that Graham's human vessel, the part of him that connects him to the life he left behind begins to fade. It is only a matter of time now before it ceases to exist completely, but not in the way that Ryan did before.

This time, he will fade into the abyss but do so with the light of Heaven behind him.

Serenity is no longer two parts of a soul torn apart, always searching for the other part. She is whole and as her eyes open and I see the flash of blue as it passes through her, her body being brought to life, glowing as her soul becomes one, she has never looked more beautiful.

My beloved has been put back together, made whole again by the very light of Heaven that we are both guided by, she is home, standing here beside me now, but more than all of that, she is something else.

She is mine.

Serenity

"How do you feel?" I hear him say as I open my eyes and take in the beauty that surrounds me.

It is a valid question. After all that I have experienced during my time on the planet, it seems fitting in a way that the first thing I am asked as everything comes together one final time is how I am. I am just not sure I have the words to express all that it is I feel.

I expected that when everything had been completed I would lose the memories of all that I have been through during my human existence, but that is not at all what has happened. I remember everything. Before I can attempt to explain all that I am experiencing though, I need to know if the way I can see things so clearly in my mind is going to be taken from me.

"The memories, will I lose them?"

"No, angelo ragazza, you will never lose them. I would never allow it."

That is interesting to me. He does not want me to forget Graham or the time that I spent with Ryan. I suppose this is something I am going to have to get used to as I am still remembering what it feels like to be human. Any new relationship that is formed usually means leaving lovers of the past behind. Gabriel not wanting that for me is hard to understand.

"You expected that I would want them taken from you?"

"Can you fault me for thinking that way? I only have human experience to go on. I know that I would not want to remember past lovers when entering into a new union with another."

"We are not like any other beings before us Serenity. What you experienced with Graham and Ryan could have easily been erased after Father brought you together, but I requested that it not happen that way. I want you the way that you are."

I can sense his truth. His heart, it speaks to mine. It is the sweetest music I have ever heard. This angel has seen my flaws, the mistakes I have made and does not wish for me to be anything other than what I have always been.

"There is something I must ask you."

"You can ask me anything, Gabriel."

"During our time together, I did things that had disastrous results. I made choices, thought things that a being of Heaven should never think. Throughout all of that, no matter how it appeared, you never gave up on me. I changed and you still stand here now despite it. If you can accept me and my flaws, why is it so hard to believe that I would do the same with you?"

I have no answer for that. He's right. I pushed him away at points, not believing in him the way I should have, choosing instead to only see what was in front of my face and not the larger picture, but even doing that, I never truly gave up on him. I always believed underneath that he was the pure being he had been from the start. I saw the light in him always, even if I didn't want to.

Letting me retain my memories with Ryan and Graham, he is accepting me, flaws and all. We really are different than all other beings before us because we are the first of our kind to realize that even a being born of the light has the ability to falter and make mistakes.

We are a new version of Heaven.

"Graham did say it best, Serenity."

"What do you mean?"

"You were his heaven. I do not believe he understood the gravity of that statement at the time, but I see it now. We are indeed a second coming of Heaven. We're going to change things together, make it better than it has ever been."

"How can you be so sure of that?"

"You saved the world from the darkness. How can you not see that with or without me you have the power to bring about a new way of being?"

"Because I am merely one person."

"You are more than just a person, Serenity. You are the brightest ball of light, the purest angel in existence. Through you, anything is possible. There's another way I know it to be the truth though. May I show you?"

Nodding, he moves closer, bringing me into him and its then I see what he's saying. The light that has until now surrounded us individually, it's different now. It's larger, more intense and bright than it had ever been during our times of separation. It is one unique light instead of two.

We are one being.

"You are my beloved and together, the possibilities are endless. Our life together, it begins now, so there is only one final thing I need to know before we begin."

"What is that?"

"Will you join me in creating an even better Heaven?"

"There is nothing I would like more, Gabriel."

It was in that moment, as I agreed to create a new, more glorious home that our lights came together, never to be separated again.

What I believed so long ago, it's never been truer than it is now.

You are never truly in darkness. Sometimes, all you need to do is turn on the light.

I'm living proof.

The End

My Heaven Playlist

Picture Perfect by Escape The Fate
In Loving Memory by Alter Bridge
Alone In This Bed (Capeside) by Framing Hanley
A Drop In The Ocean by Ron Pope
Let Me Go by Avril Lavigne
Holding On To Heaven by Nickelback
Demons by Brian McFadden
My Immortal by Evanescence
Only You're The One by Lifehouse
Dear Agony by Breaking Benjamin
Without You by Breaking Benjamin
Love Remains The Same by Gavin Rossdale
Into Your Arms by The Maine
Anthem Of The Angels by Breaking Benjamin
Your Guardian Angel by The Red Jumpsuit Apparatus
Call And Answer by Barenaked Ladies
Soulmate by Natasha Bedingfield
Tangled Up In You by Staind
Wake Up by Framing Hanley
I'll Fight by Daughtry
Wherever You Will Go by The Calling
Nothing Like Starting Over by Hunter Hayes

Acknowledgements

Caleb, Noah, Raine and Isabella. Thank you for being my four real life angels. I wouldn't be able to be me or do this without you. Mommy loves you.

Joey. You pushed for this, so this book especially is yours. Thank you for pushing me to explore this. You'll never know how much I treasure that and you. I love you.

Daddy. I can't have acknowledgements without you. You and Mom believed in me when no one else even knew I existed. Thank you for being my biggest fans before I even knew what the word fan meant.

Pamela Sparkman. Meeting you and getting to read your tremendous story of love and hope has been such a blessing to me. Thank you, not only for being a friend but for sharing your love story with the world. I'm honored to call you friend.

Linda, Mallory and Zach. I could easily call you my second family, but you're more than that. You are all honorary Winchesters and my first family. I love you all. Thank you for making the world, my world so bright and full of love and light.

To everyone that reads my work. Thank you as always for spending your hard earned money and time with my stories and for leaving me the feedback you have on it. You will never know how much that and you mean to me. I love you all.

About The Author

Melyssa Winchester is a mother of four from Toronto, Ontario, Canada. When she's not knee deep in adolescent awesomeness, she's falling in love, one book boyfriend and girlfriend at a time. She is a lover of all things romance and will forever believe in a real and true happily ever after.

When she's not off being a mom or writing you can find her doing one of two things. Reading or buried under the covers watching Supernatural, Sons of Anarchy or Veronica Mars.

Melyssa is currently working on Before The Light Book #3 Iridescent Vengeance (Lucifer's Story) that follows the lives of the characters from the Love United Series before they came together. She is also hard at work on a standalone title Shades of Blue and plotting many more upcoming projects for the future.

You can find her on the web, either at her personal site, Facebook (which she just might have an obsession with) or Twitter (@WinchesterBooks) where she talks incessantly about her kids, her writing and all things book boyfriend related.

www.ingramcontent.com/pod-product-compliance
Lightning Source LLC
Chambersburg PA
CBHW070829120626
46556CB00002B/687